THE FOURTH LEVEL
HOSTILE TAKEOVER
BOOK ONE

NICHOLAS HUNTLEY

"Misunderstanding and neglect occasion more mischief in the world than even malice and wickedness."

– Johann Wolfgang von Goethe

Act 1, Scene 1

The morning that came was just like any other in the rural Albertan town of Allabrese. The sun crept over the large dry hills to cast its light onto the quiet and peaceful town that rested upon the plateau. Allabrese looked down to the many farms, houses, and ranches of the local townspeople like the Acropolis. The golden cast continued its stretch beyond and down to the sand and shingle beaches with overgrown grass reaching high before moving onto the crystalline water of the Nattau River that simmered peacefully before reaching the coast on the other side.

A large manor house sat beyond the shore road on the opposite side, above the short beachhead cliffs. It had a wide semi-circular driveway that drove past the pointed steel-black gates and surrounding perimeter fence up to the front of the mansion at the top of the short hill. The warm rays rested upon the house to give the exterior tan brick walls the mere string of life it could attain. To the side was dense mixture of forest that acted as a border before moving beyond to the rolling plains and farmland past.

Cabernet Manor, as it was called, rested proudly on the opposite bank from Allabrese with its Edwardian architecture. There, on the front driveway, a luxurious black sedan pulled up and ceased her engine at the base of the stairs to the front of the mansion. The stairs came up to a platform protected by three arches of clean chiseled stone. Behind the arches was the front entrance.

The driver of the car opened the driver's seat door and the man pulled his designer Italian black leather shoes out to step on the flagstone that composed the driveway. The man closed the door behind him and walked to the rear of the car to open the trunk. He stood over the compartment with his grey tweed trousers, and matching suit jacket and vest. He bent forward to pick up two brown paper bags filled with the same fruit from the local grocers.

An apricot fell from the many as he hugged the two bags with each arm. The fruit landed at his feet and rolled towards the left rear tire. The man closed the trunk and walked around to lean over and carefully pick up the apricot as he pressed the bags in his arms against his chest. He scooped the fruit out with his pale-boney hands, almost denting his golden Swiss watch along the flagstone. He stood back up afterwards and began to climb up the three-step stairs to the landing and before one of the two oak doors entering the mansion.

The man turned around from the entrance to expose his fine-silver hair to the morning sunlight and looked through his aged blue eyes at the fresh sunrise. He turned back around and fiddled with his keys to open one of the main doors to the house before pushing the set back to enter the void front entrance. The foyer was one of the largest rooms in the house. Its walls were a cherry wood panel that crept up to the crème white paint above. At the immediate left of the front door was a coat hanger in the corner. To the right was a wooden table with an expensive vase atop.

At the back of the room were tall-arched Versailles windows that looked into the back patio with Egyptian white cotton curtains hung and closed. Both left and right led to separate wide staircases that went upwards, hiding most of the rear of the foyer behind them. In the middle space was a large crimson red rectangular carpet that stretched from the entrance to the patio windows, and then from staircase to staircase. At the anterior side of the right staircase was an old white linen cushioned chair with a table of the same wood at its right side.

Atop the table was a porcelain vase with a single, long, but dead sunflower. At the anterior side of left staircase was a similar setup, but with a telephone atop the table instead of a vase.

Behind the left staircase, out of sight, was a white frame glass window door leading to the patio. On the wall adjacent was a portrait covered under a white sheet. Light barely shined into the dimly lit foyer and despite it being late spring, the room – or entire house, was cold.

The man turned right through an open arched doorway that led into the next room. The arch mimicked the same one on the exact opposite left wall that led into short corridor going into the south wing of the house.

The room that the man had turned into, which was the living room, one could walk diagonally, continuing into a corridor before turning west to enter a larger room before the ballroom. To the man's left was a plain wall with an old telephone against the wall and a white-blinded door that led into a guest bathroom. To the right was a nook with curtained windows that looked out to the driveway and beyond. Each of the lateral walls of this nook had some sort of loveseat with white sheets overtop.

Old family portraits and paintings were neatly and politely hung around the olive-colored walls. Alternative to the continuing corridor was another open doorway ahead, behind one of the couches, leading into a dining room.

This alcove was more of a dinette than a proper dining room due to the small round table in the middle. The room itself had a medieval appearance with stone walls and tiles. Each corner was decorated with a plant that was slowly withering away. In the middle of the room was a small chandelier with webs netting around and large arched windows were arranged along every wall that looked outside

The man continued through the house and around another arched entryway to enter a small vestibule with merely a small table on the right. He entered through a dark oak door and came to the kitchen.

The bags of groceries were set atop of the white marble counters. The house kitchen was not large, nor was it small. A half-height arched window was perched to the left. The view looked down to the extended driveway that sloped from the main loop to the garage annex. The counters of the kitchen were split between the white tops and light birchwood bottoms that matched the cabinets over top. Ahead, between two doors on the other side of the room, was a refrigerator whose emptiness noted signs of a non-existent famine. In the middle of the kitchen was an island with stoves on the side facing away from the man. A rack of pots and pans hung over the island.

The door on the left of the refrigerator led into the large room before the ballroom, which was a foyer with empty cabinets and pedestals. The door on the right led into a storeroom. The storeroom led immediately towards a freight elevator that could only descend from this room.

Two large plastic bags of apricots rose from the brown paper bags and were laid onto the counter. One of the two bags had its knot undone until the man retied it so that both were equal. He let the bags rest on the counter as he walked over to the sink nearby. He opened the cabinet above and retrieved a black plastic bowl. Inside the bowl was an apple, which was separated from where it was to be washed in the sink. The man then took a large bite from the apple, causing some of its juices to spill from his lips and enter the confines of his neatly groomed moustache that only extended as far as his upper lip went.

With the bags of apricots in his arms, he left the kitchen with the bowl and came to the main entrance of the house again. He walked up the staircase to reach the ledge that surrounded the foyer from the second floor and also gave a direct view of the large brass chandelier in the center of the room. The man then left the foyer, walking into north wing again. He entered a miniature foyer that extended into a long corridor going west. This part of the house was an ancient and unused sector with only one room that served a real purpose for the principal inhabitant, the man. He looked down this corridor with a pensive face and slightly sad look before going to the first door on his right, along a diagonal wall to enter the room directly above the dinette.

The room on the other side was a makeshift laboratory. On the immediate right of the man was the workbench where he once assembled a miniature rocket. The surface now held various incomplete projects as well as boxes of loose scrap metal. On the immediate left was a table with a cutting board, various empty flasks, test tubes, and distilling equipment. Underneath this table were several boxes with various containers containing different types of compounds as well as some tanks with a variety of gases. The wall adjacent to the table was a door with a large window in the middle that looked onto the small terrace with an amateur hobby telescope sat. Besides the door was another table with an old monitor and computer sitting on top that used an operating system he had completed himself. Underneath the table, in front of the stool, was a mini-fridge that contained anything but edible goods. Next to it, at the back of the room was a large cylindrical chamber he designed himself that was hooked up to the computer. Besides the apparatus was another table with a microscope, small storage compartments, and glass cages that once held many lively specimens, but were now devoid of life. On the adjacent wall was a model of a human skeleton and a door leading into the small bathroom with a converted shower for emergencies, a sink, and a toilet for convenience.

The man walked forward to the empty table in the middle of the room and dropped the bag of apricots on top before turning around to close and look at the door that he came through just now. On the back of the door laid a hook that hung his well-kept lab coat. He laid one hand on the fibers of the coat's left sleeve before removing it from its hook and taking a look at tag along the neck of the jacket. He examined the coat while he held a blank face as though he was lost in his thoughts.

The man read the name stitched along the left breast of the jacket in a quiet voice, "Charlemagne de la Cabernet."

Charlemagne put his lab coat on and walked over to the chemistry station to find his safety glasses and a butcher's knife. He walked back to the table and began to remove the apricots one by one. He laid apricot after apricot onto the cutting board before starting to cut each one to extract their seed. He discarded the fruit back into the bowl while he kept the seeds on top of the original plastic bags for ease of organization.

The seeds were perfect for Charlemagne's intentions. Once he had finished cutting the apricots, he grabbed a pair of plyers and began to crack the shells open for the small almond-like kernel inside. He did so for each apricot seed before taking all the shells and throwing them out in a garbage bin underneath the middle table. With the small bits of the insides in a pile, he began to take the butcher's knife to cut every piece into smaller digits before gently placing all of them in a medium-sized, round flask. He then took the flask and entered the washroom to fill the glass with water. He then took the jar to his chemistry station and rested the flask upon a stand over a small Bunsen burner. Charlemagne then took an extended fractioning column (a tall glass container to capture and condense the vapor) and attached it to the top of a condenser with its end pointing to a beaker.

Charlemagne took a flint lighter and a small container from the boxes underneath the table with a spoon in the other hand. He turned the valve of the Bunsen burner that was connected to a tank of methane under the table, opened the container to take a tablespoon of citric acid out and dissolved it within the water with the bits of apricot kernels. Once everything was set, Charlemagne took a step back to let the water boil while he went over to clean up the mess on the middle table. He took the fruit and dumped them in a plastic container with no intention of eating them at a later date. Charlemagne then took the plastic bags and threw them into the garbage bin in the bathroom before he walked over to the curtains and closed them to block the vivid sunlight from entering the laboratory. Charlemagne then took a chance to raise his hands over his mouth and let out a broad yawn before walking around to take a seat at the middle table.

Charlemagne waited for the reflux extraction to complete, but this would take time. He paced anxiously in the room before he went downstairs to cook and eat. Once he was fed, he returned upstairs to shut the valve of the natural gas tank and turn the Bunsen burner off. He took the beaker and walked over to the large apparatus in the far-left corner of the room and began to remove the mush that he had isolated. He then placed this isolated content into a test tube. Charlemagne then went over to an apparatus in the corner of the room, tapping on a console for a tray to extend out of the apparatus for him to insert the tube. Next, Charlemagne walked over to the computer beside the apparatus and began to fiddle with some settings to release the purring of the machine beside him before the rotor of the drive began to slowly spin in centrifuge. Once the machine began to roar, he looked onto his computer screen and shut off the monitor before moving his hands over his mouth to let out another much-needed yawn. He then stood up from his desk and walked around the room carefully only to have himself grown even more tired. The room had darkened now that the sun was shining on the other side of the mansion, which didn't help Charlemagne stay awake.

Charlemagne began to put his elbows onto his desk and slouch over his keyboard as he rested his head with patience. With one last look to the machine in front of him, he began to close his tired eyes. With sharp breaths, the day was ending for Charlemagne – this was a time for ends. With one last deep breath, Charlemagne de la Cabernet fell into a deep sleep with the light buzzing of the apparatus next to him, moaning in the background as his subconscious drifted, for tomorrow would truly bring about the end of an era.

Act 1, Scene 2

The obnoxious jingle of the front doorbell went off. Charlemagne rushed his head up from the keyboard and brought his right hand up to the right-side of his face as he attempted to recollect himself. He then stood up from his stool and looked around the makeshift laboratory in confusion. The machine was quiet. Sunlight poked out from behind the curtains.

Charlemagne walked over to a window looking out at the front entrance and tried to get a view of who was ringing the doorbell. The sun was rising from the east. It was a new morning. Charlemagne cringed as the doorbell went off for him again in its arrhythmic tone. He left the lab and went downstairs to rush to the door. Charlemagne put his hands over the door handles and opened the doors quickly to see who was there.

A man in a cheap grey suit stood in front of him. He was of fair skin with an earpiece in his right ear, clipboard in his right hand, and with slicked back brown hair almost in a mullet. The other person next to him was much shorter – about an entire half a foot shorter than Charlemagne who was six feet tall. Charlemagne looked at the child, or perhaps, adolescent. She had a suitcase pulled up behind her and an unpleasant look upon her face that refused to look straight at Charlemagne as it was instead turned to the side into the bushes beside them.

The girl had long dark hair, which was messy and untidy. She had a fine jawline and tender pale face that held tired blue eyes. She wore a denim vest over a white t-shirt and jeans, which gave her an impoverished look in addition to her slim figure.

"Can I help you?" Charlemagne quietly asked in his East Anglian accent.

"Charlemagne de la Cabernet," the man in the suit greeted. "It's me! Chris – Christopher Macintyre with British Columbia Child Services. Do you remember me? I certainly remember you – I left a message this morning."

"I don't seem to understand – child services? British Columbia?" Charlemagne replied. "We're in Alberta, and, I must add, I have never met you in my life."

Macintyre produced an ID from his suit. It looked official.

"I seem to remember you very clearly, Mr. Cabernet. In fact, I can remember each and every one of our conversations very clearly. We talked face-to-face, I evaluated your penthouse, and you even signed the papers officiating the adoption on these papers," he said, showing Charlemagne own unforged signature on the adoption forms. "You requested little Diana yourself – all the way from Harlech."

"I'm not little," Diana threatened in an urban accent, turning to face him, "and I told you I don't want to be here – no less with this clueless geezer."

"I beg your pardon?" Charlemagne questioned, looking away from his clipboard.

"Fellas, listen," Macintyre cut in. "I'd love to be around for you two to bond, but I'm afraid I don't have much time to stick around. Mr. Cabernet, if you have any questions then you know how to reach me. Alternatively, you can also come back around to my offices in Victoria. Otherwise, I'm going to leave you two together and I'll call in several weeks to catch up, okay?"

Macintyre stepped back and caused Charlemagne to stutter as he panicked at a loss for words.

"W-wait!" Charlemagne said. "Come back! I can't take care of her! I – I—?!"

"You'll do fine, Mr. Cabernet!" Macintyre replied, waving his hand as he walked back around to get into his car. "Ciao, ciao, fellas!"

Charlemagne watched as the car drove off from the mansion before looking over to Diana who stood impatiently in the same spot.

"What are you looking at?" she asked as the two confronted each other.

"Is this some sort of joke?" Charlemagne asked, noticing the fragile voice the young girl had.

"I wish. I figured the worse when I was going to meet the great owner of Cabernet Industries. I got one thing right though. You're nuts."

Diana took a step forward to walk into the house. Charlemagne took a side-step to block her.

"Hold on there," Charlemagne reacted, backing her up. "Not so fast. This isn't your home."

"I know it's not," she replied. "We'll see how long this'll last before I see Mac-in-douche again to take me to a new home. I doubt it'll be more than a week."

"A week?" Charlemagne repeated in fear. "No... no. You come here now," he added, taking off his lab coat and hanging it inside.

Charlemagne stepped back out and brought the luggage in before closing the door behind him.

"We seem to be at a mutual consensus that neither of us want to be near the other. Let's go to city hall and see if we can expedite this miserable error, shall we?"

Charlemagne walked down the steps to his luxurious black sedan and unlocked the doors to step into the driver's seat. He looked over to Diana who was still at the top of the steps with her arms crossed.

"Well, come on now!" he said to her.

Diana uncrossed her arms and stepped down. She walked to the passenger seat door, opened it, and stepped in as Charlemagne started the engine of his car. Charlemagne gave a nervous glance at the girl as he thought for a moment. Diana looked at him and Charlemagne shook his head with doubt. He looked back in front of him and drove off to the gates of the estate. The gates opened for him to turn left onto the road along the coastline. He drove along and merged into an on-ramp that connected with the Nattau Bridge going over the river, which was part of the main freeway.

Diana, with little emotion (especially for the countryside imagery) looked out the passenger seat window just as she did when driving with Mr. Macintyre in the taxi from the airfield. The rural arena around her was vastly different from the modern city she was familiar with. Diana frowned at the difference. Farms of crops extended up to downtown Allabrese on either side of the freeway once off the bridge. It was everything she had come to expect and dread when she learned she was being taken to Alberta – no less – a town she had never read or heard of.

Charlemagne continued to drive as he came into the small suburban outskirts of the small town before making his way to the downtown sector where the town cinema, library, Cabernet Industries historic and current head offices were, and most importantly, city hall could be found. He drove to the city center where Allabrese Central Park was dashed behind Main Street to look onto the Allabrese Civic Centre, otherwise known as city hall. Charlemagne turned right from the freeway and onto Main Street where he pulled over in front of the pathway into the main entrance of the large mansion that had been converted into the town civic center. Charlemagne looked at the heritage site before looking at Diana before him with disgust. Diana looked back at him with a look of equal disgust.

"Get me out of here, gramps," Diana said as she got out.

"Stop calling out my age," Charlemagne protested as he opened his door. "I'll have you know that I'm merely in my fifties!"

"Doesn't make that much of a difference, but thanks for the info anyways," Diana sarcastically replied.

Diana got out of the car as Charlemagne walked around to step on the sidewalk. The two joined each other to walk up the path to the main doors. Charlemagne opened the door for Diana before entering himself into the lobby of the municipal center. Both of them stepped forward to the furthest oak desk in the back of the elegant foyer.

The entrance was different from that of Cabernet Manor. It was pinkish-brown with its rose carpet, royal magenta walls and gold chandelier. A set of stairs were on either side, like in Cabernet Manor, but in the very back instead of the middle to go up to the second floor. Four wooden desks (two on each side) were in the entrance with filing cabinets and tables with piles of documents behind them. There was only one secretary present this morning.

The woman, Dorothy by her nametag, was young and had semi-circle glasses that clipped into her bun-tied hair. She wore a warm yellow blouse over a brown skirt and was busy filing her fingernails as she relaxed her elbows on the pile of work in front of her.

"Mr. Cabernet?" she greeted with a tame smile. "How can I help somebody like yourself?"

"I need to see child services," Charlemagne quickly requested.

"Oh," she replied, looking over to the little teen that was behind him. "I didn't realize that you, uh… had a kid, or were married for that matter."

"I'm not his kid," Diana quickly corrected.

"She's not mine," Charlemagne affirmed, "and I'm," he chuckled over top, "not married for that matter either, thank you very much."

"Of course," the woman replied without much care. "Well, you'll want the third door on the right upstairs. You can't miss it," she said, pointing up the right staircase with her nail file. "I'll let Mr. Gregson know you're here."

"Thank you," Charlemagne said.

Diana glared at the woman over this offence before following Charlemagne up the stairs. The two of them came to the third door on the right where there was a door with a bronze plaque sign that read, "Family Services."

Charlemagne knocked on the door and stepped back as it opened to reveal a bald man in a banana yellow dress shirt with the sleeves rolled up. He had a matching brown tie.

"Mr. Cabernet?" the man asked, squinting through his black glasses.

"Hello," Charlemagne greeted. "I need to have a word about a recent 'adoption' placed under me… no doubt by mistake might I add."

"You're the mistake, old man," Diana muttered.

Charlemagne heard but tried to ignore her words as he grinded his teeth together. Diana noticed it by the way his jaws tensed. The balding man looked down at Diana and then over to Charlemagne as he stepped back and Charlemagne let himself in.

"Right. Of course, Mr. Cabernet. Please, have a seat."

The man walked into his own office and around his desk to sit down. The office was small, but lit. It was messy with a single filing cabinet in the back and various legal boxes scattered and piled around. Diana looked at the name plate at the front of the desk that read the man's full name: Roger Gregson. Charlemagne sat down and crossed his arms and legs as he laid back impatiently.

"You say that this girl was placed under your care 'mistakenly?'" Gregson questioned.

"That's correct. A man all the way from British Columbia came to my front door to unload this *child* into my care. I thought he was out of his mind – I thought this was some sort of joke, but for some peculiar reason, he had my signature! It was all set and done! I had never even met the man before in my life – but he claimed that he had met me!"

"Right, just calm down, Mr. Cabernet," Gregson replied, pausing for a moment as he looked at his computer screen before back at the two. "British Columbia, huh?"

"I thought it was quite peculiar myself. After all, the lass is from Harlech. I haven't been to Harlech in at least a year and a half!"

"This *lass* has a name!" Diana snarled.

"What's your name, love?" Gregson asked, trying to be warm."

"Diana," she replied. "Diana Cambridge."

"Alright then, Diana," Gregson replied, turning his chair to his computer.

The computer looked as though it was from the last century.

"Well, this sounds peculiar, Charles," the public servant continued to say. "Have you checked with any of your representatives? It's strange that the provincial government of B.C. would let you adopt from them given that you're an Albertan resident by address. I have honestly no idea how this could have happened. It's the first case I've ever come across in terms of a 'mistake.'"

"Please...! Please tell me there is something – anything that you can do! I can't have this burden on me at this moment. I'm a busy man and have – oh, damn! That's right. I have (or at least had) a plane to catch for Harlech! I must be at Cabernet Tower for some important negotiations...!"

"Oof... well, I wish there was some sort of short-term solution I could offer you, Mr. Cabernet, but with a situation like this, I'm afraid we can only look at the long-term. We're in Alberta. Had this been a matter with our own government then this would be a different matter, but, uh... that's not the case. What was the name of the man that dropped Diana into your care?"

"Christopher Macintyre," Charlemagne answered with a bitterness in his voice.

Charlemagne took out a business card that Macintyre had given to him. He gave it to Gregson.

"Right..." Gregson replied, taking the card and writing it on a sticky note alongside Diana's name.

"I'll tell you two what. Let me have a word with the boys in Victoria to figure out what is going on, and I'll get back to you as soon as I can," Gregson said.

"What about the girl?" Charlemagne questioned with high hope.

"We live far from any foster homes, Mr. Cabernet. Our little town has a mere two-thousand people. You know that. You're our biggest employer between the office complex and laboratories over on Champion Plains. These types of things take time, and to find a place for Diana has a load of legal tape that I can't cross until I hear from the B.C. government and learn more about what is going on."

Gregson paused for a moment as his body faced the two of them, but his face at his computer screen. He held a pen horizontally in front of him from both sides, pinching each side as he thought.

"The best I can estimate is two months," Gregson concluded.

"Two months?!" Charlemagne and Diana reacted with distaste.

"You can't be serious.... You mean I'm stuck with *him* in this hell for that long!" Diana questioned, breathing a little too quickly.

"No, that can't be right," Charlemagne replied, sitting back as he gained a nervous laugh. "I'm hallucinating. This isn't real. The girl is right. I'm in hell. I can't be responsible for her for two months... I'm not a parent."

"I'm sorry about this situation, Mr. Cabernet," Gregson responded, "but if what the B.C. government has done is right, then I'm sure you were very eligible to raise a daughter of your own. The process alone is extensive, and you must have some memory of going through with this – the home inspection... the interviews and background checks. Even for a celebrity like yourself, it is no walk in the park. You're all treated the same in the system. Are you *sure* you don't remember anything?!"

"Are you accusing me of being senile?!" Charlemagne charged. "I mean," he added, calming down, "I have thought of adoption before... but I never went through with it. Something came up in my life, and even then, I don't remember paying a dime!"

"I'm not accusing you of anything, Mr. Cabernet," Gregson reasoned, raising a palm to him. "I'll do what I can as I realize you are upset. A man that does not want to raise a daughter is not eligible to be a father--"

"Ain't that the truth..." Diana muttered.

"--I'll do what I can to alleviate you of this... 'burden' as you describe into a more suitable family."

"Been there, done that," Diana commented.

"This *will* take time, however," Gregson stressed. "Until then, I'm afraid I'll need to keep both you and Diana in Allabrese for ease of contact. Neither of you can leave the province until we've cleared settled this matter."

"What? You're grounding us? No!" Charlemagne reacted. "You can't ground us – I have business to attend in Harlech! I... I..."

"You're the chairman of one of the largest companies worldwide and a busy billionaire, but it's the only way to ensure two months don't extend into a year. In the meantime, get accustomed to raising Diana like your own daughter--"

"Ha!" Diana shouted.

Diana looked at both the adults embarrassingly and backed into her chair. Gregson and Charlemagne both looked at her before looking at each other. Gregson looked down and opened a desk drawer. He reached inside, took out some pamphlets, and pushed them over to Charlemagne.

"Accept responsibility and be a father for a couple of months..." Gregson said.

Charlemagne looked at the pamphlets as if they were something foreign to him. He picked one up and read the title. Each brochure was optimistic in appearance with happy couples and their children. He looked away from pamphlet and over to the grumpy girl next to him.

Gregson wrote something on the same sticky note before removing it and placing it underneath his monitor. He then opened another desk drawer and removed a business card from it. He wrote something on the back of it before pushing it to Charlemagne.

"I've opened a case and will get to work on this right now. Until I get word from Victoria, I'll be in touch with regular checkups, understood?"

Gregson stood up and extended his hand to bid the two farewell.

"Yes, of course..." Charlemagne replied in a quiet tone.

Charlemagne shook Mr. Gregson's hand as he rose from his chair. Diana snubbed him and stood up after Charlemagne had left the room. She walked behind Charlemagne as they went down the hall towards the stairs. Charlemagne ignored the secretary as he walked past her and turned to head out the front door.

"Have a nice afternoon, Mr. Cabernet," the secretary said as she waved to him.

Diana looked at her displeasingly before turning and continuing to follow Charlemagne. Charlemagne stepped into a light spring rain that was hitting the downtown area. He raised the brochures in his hand over his head at the shower of rain hit his white hairs. Charlemagne then looked over to Diana as she joined him at his side. She simply stood in the rain with a somber face that looked to the side, away from Charlemagne's as she examined her surroundings with crossed arms. The bells of the clock tower above them struck and chimed. It was almost noon.

"Come on," Charlemagne sighed in the same quiet tone. "Let's go."

Act 1, Scene 3

Charlemagne's car began to pull into Cabernet Manor from their trip downtown as the rain started to pick up into a heavy downpour within the ten-minute drive. Charlemagne raised the parking brake, shifted gears and turned off the car engine. The life in the engine shut off, leaving both Diana and Charlemagne alone in silence with the patter of rain hitting the sides of the sedan. Diana still held the same frown and crossed arms as earlier. She continued to look to the side, ignoring Charlemagne as she brooded in the solitude of her own mind.

Charlemagne made the first move and opened his car door. He stepped out as he exposed his left leg to the rain. He closed the door behind him as the passenger seat door opened for Diana to come out. Charlemagne walked around the car and passed her to go up the steps towards the front doors to open them. He unlocked the door and opened it to step in. He stopped as he looked at the luggage, sighed and then turned to the girl.

"Oh God, how could this have happened to me...?" Charlemagne muttered under his breath as the girl took her time to enter the house.

Diana was soaking wet as she entered the mansion. She walked to her luggage and grabbed the handle.

"Let's, err... let's bring your things to a bedroom upstairs, shall we?" Charlemagne said as the rain pounded on the manor rooftops in ambience.

"Why even bother," Diana pessimistically replied, picking up her backpack as well before following Charlemagne. "I'm not sticking around."

Charlemagne ignored her and instead led her to the right staircase. They made it to the top before walking over to a doorway leading into the north wing of the house. They entered a small foyer between the main entrance, hallway to the left, and a door on a diagonal wall on the right (leading into the makeshift lab). The two of them walked into the left hall and came to the first door on the right.

Charlemagne opened the door and entered a void room with a brown carpet, dirty white walls and two tall windows at the opposite wall from the door. There was also a door next to the windows on the right.

"Uh... maybe not this bedroom," Charlemagne remarked with discomfort. "I'll give you two options."

Diana looked into the room as Charlemagne moved forward. She felt a worrisome chill. They passed the third door and went straight to the fourth and last one at the end of the hall. The end of the hall had a window that looked into a small patio veranda and French window that led into the room before the door in front of them. Charlemagne put his hand over the brass doorknob that he once used to turn regularly and began to turn it again and push through.

Charlemagne walked into the plain bedroom with light blue walls, a double bed stripped of any sheets in a dark-brown frame in the far-left corner with a similar-colored desk beside it, and a similar-colored dresser on the immediate right of Charlemagne and Diana next to an entrenched closet. The two walked into the room where Diana let go of her luggage as she looked around with a more neutral face than she held earlier. There were two windows behind the bed, and two on the left-side wall making four in total (excluding the French window).

"This is your other option to the former room I showed you," Charlemagne said. "Does this suit you better?"

Diana looked over to the French window and then to the door next to the dresser. Charlemagne looked at that door too.

"Oh, yes. It has a bathroom adjacent, which also goes into a different empty room with no windows, which also goes into your first option. They're all interconnected," Charlemagne explained.

Diana gave no response.

"Well, I'll let you decide," Charlemagne concluded. "There should be some clean white sheets in the laundry room."

Diana continued to give no response as she looked around the foreign room. She had never had such a large room to herself before. To her, it felt strange to think that this was all hers, at least, for the time being. The room was nearly as big as the small apartment she used to live in the slums of Harlech. Diana looked around again and then over to the French window. She walked over to look into the small patio as she felt a little homesick with the rain that mimicked Harlech's rude weather. She then looked over to Charlemagne who was still in the room.

Diana thought about the strange, old geezer that she had just met in the little hours that had passed. She didn't like him and thought it was odd that this business mogul was her guardian for the time being. She was also cautious and suspicious at the same time. It felt wrong to be in this house. She also felt neglected by Charlemagne at the same time, despite her intentions and desire to leave, by his own desire to rid her. His desire was sooner than what her latest foster parents had felt about her. The entire ordeal made Diana feel disconnected over her temporary housing. Then again, Diana also thought and knew that any house to come could never feel like the home she used to reign sovereign in.

Charlemagne stepped to the door at the end of the right wall and opened it to reveal the decaying ancient bathroom that had been ripped apart due to Charlemagne's tinkering. The showers had been torn from the pipes behind the wall. A dirty hole filled with murky water existed in the floor where the toilet must have been. Only a corner tub remained alongside a porcelain sink, which itself had been smashed on the left-side and thus completely unusable. Diana looked around the bathroom and began to reminisce in the closet bathroom at her old home, which was equally distasteful and in dire need for repair.

"I'll call for some renovation to be done later today," Charlemagne said as he looked at the mess. "I doubt we can do anything about this until tomorrow though. In the meanwhile, you are free to use the bathroom downstairs near the sitting parlor."

"Yeah, whatever," Diana replied, trying to conceal her inner thoughts.

Charlemagne looked over to the girl as she left him and went to her luggage.

"I'm not a chef when it comes to cooking," Charlemagne also said. "If you get to be peckish, then feel free to order out. There are phonebooks by the telephone in the main entrance. I'll be around to answer the door and pay. Just please remember to order me something as well if you could... if it isn't too much to ask."

Diana turned to look at Charlemagne behind her. Her stomach growled. She had forgotten how hungry she had been and how she had been travelling for the last couple of hours. All she had for breakfast today was some oatmeal and toast that she was given. She didn't reply to him or even nod. She simply went back to messing around with her luggage as she anxiously waited for Charlemagne to leave her be.

Charlemagne took the hint and left. Diana looked to the door as he walked out and turned to go down the hall. She took the opportunity to close the door behind him and leave herself in peace. She picked up her backpack, walked over to the stripped mattress, and sat down with it on her lap.

"What now?" Diana whispered to herself, looking around and through the many curtain-less windows in the bedroom.

Diana put her backpack to her side and stood up. She walked over to the French window and stood an inch from the glass. She opened the door and let in a warm breeze from outside into the chilled room. She walked onto the small veranda to take a look at the rear of the mansion.

Cabernet Manor was not a large estate by its structure, but instead its terrain. The building consisted of two two-story wings between the central foyer. Behind the foyer was a large terrace with a swimming pool in the center. The entirety of the section extended ahead of the house and then dropped into two separate stairwells that connected and led together to the gardens below.

The mansion had a large garden sector filled with various blooming flowers. Diana looked ahead to the garden and gave notice to the three separate sections within the gardens. The furthest section behind the south wing of the house (opposite from Diana) was the smallest due to a large but shallow pond with a fountain spraying water in a circle. There was a small patio that extended from the center of the garden with barricades left, right and the opposite side from the pond. On the same opposite-side there was an arched arbor in the middle. Around the barricades were shrubs of roses in bloom.

The center of the garden was simple, but the largest section with a traditional stone waterfall fountain situated in the middle. Chiseled stone benches stood on either side. The border of the center garden was filled with vibrant shrubbery, blooming flowers, and a surrounding pathway. The sector behind Diana's room was wider and extended away from this side of the north wing. It was a simple pathway headed to a fence with flowers and shrubs on either side.

The entire area behind the garden was a wide field that wasn't marked by any visible fencing from where Diana stood. It must have continued for at least a kilometer or two. Beyond that, the field turned into a forest, and behind this forest were the Rocky Mountains.

Diana gave the entire area another glimpse. She found comfort in the rain for another moment before stepping back, turning, and going back into her bedroom. She walked across it and towards the oak desk to lean over and look out the window.

Behind this wall was a drop down to a fenced dirt enclosure with empty trots filled with rainwater. She also saw an annex extending from the mansion behind one of the rooms next to the bathroom (not hers though). It was two-stories tall with very wide, but rustic garage doors. Diana looked back at the pen. It seemed to her as though there should have been animals in the enclosure.

Diana closed away from the desk and went over to her luggage. She thought about moving some of her stuff, but then again, she didn't have much in her possession. Instead, she simply left it there and walked to the doorway out of this miserable room. She opened it, stepped out, and closed the door behind her.

The house may have well have been haunted with the white sheets over the furniture. Then again, even ghosts might have been more life than the current inhabitants. Diana made it to the end of the hall and walked over to the door of the diagonal wall. She put her hand around the doorknob only to struggle to open it. She gave a mean look as she stepped back and her curiosity soared to know what was behind this door. However, it immediately dropped as she figured it might be Charlemagne's bedroom.

Diana gave the door one last look before turning around to go through the door into the deck around the main foyer. She put her hands along the railing next to the staircase and looked down. Diana glanced at a lone table beside the opposite stairway that had a lamp, telephone and phonebooks atop. A white sheet covered the chair next to it. She also looked over to the closest front entrance of the house and noticed piles of newspapers atop of one another that had been collected for however long. Diana finally set her hands away from the railing and stepped over to go down the stairs. She looked around the main entrance and up at the chandelier above. She closed her eyes and took a long deep breath before exhaling as she opened them.

"I'm not in Harlech anymore, am I..." she said to herself.

•

Diana and Charlemagne both sat awkwardly with each other in the dining room as they ate their lunch in silence together. Diana didn't even bother to look up to Charlemagne – not out of spite or to snub him. Charlemagne looked at the long frown that Diana gave as she looked down at her half-finished food. The silence continued, especially as Charlemagne washed his plate in the kitchen. He could feel the cold stare of Diana standing at the opposite end of the room as he began to dry both plates. Once he finished, he turned around to look at her.

"Have you had the chance to look around?" Charlemagne asked in a stern voice.

"No," she responded in a plain tone.

"Let me show you around then," Charlemagne sighed, walking towards one of three doors in the kitchen.

Charlemagne approached the door on the right from where he was standing, opened the swinging door, and held it for Diana as she came over and went through. Diana walked ahead and past Charlemagne with a frown as they entered end of the hall from the sitting parlor. It was a medium-sized room with pedestals, cabinets, and display cases alongside another French window leading towards the patio on the right-side and a white door on the furthest.

Diana emotionlessly looked around the room, not even bothering to examine the little trophies or valuables that existed and could be hocked. Instead, she followed Charlemagne as he held the white door for her.

Charlemagne entered after her, and the two examined the largest room in the mansion with its marble-checkered floor and elegant crimson walls. Versailles windows occupied every possible side. It was the most decorated room in the mansion with suits of armor, the Cabernet family banner, and paintings still left around. A bar could be seen at the back but was devoid of supply. A wooden table sat lonely against the left wall on its side.

"The parties used to be held here in the ballroom," Charlemagne said to her.

Diana looked around before stepping back into the trophy room with Charlemagne. Together, they walked down the hall and into the parlor. Charlemagne pointed to a door to the right of them.

"This is the bathroom you can use until someone takes care of the old one upstairs... if it gets done. I'm not sure yet."

"Great," Diana sarcastically and quietly whispered.

The two left the north wing of the house and walked into the main foyer to head across into the opposing wing – the south wing. They entered another hallway that went down and had a single door to choose from on the opposite end from them. Charlemagne put his hand on the knob and turned it to enter a large two-story chamber.

Diana entered behind him and paused as he took in what he saw. Her eyes immediately met the large bookcases alongside the right-side of the room, underneath a loft above with small chandeliers dangling from underneath – it all caused the muscles in his face to trigger a shy smile. Diana looked away from the bookcases for a second, glancing at the wooden spiral staircase for a moment and then looking at the two desks conjoined together, but with no chairs or substances atop. His eyes shifted from the back of the room and towards the center where two brown sofas faced each other with a large carpet underneath and a large chandelier directly above.

Diana stepped ahead of Charlemagne as she walked inside to get a better view. The middle of the left wall had a tall and wide window that poured what little light was outside and into the library. On his immediate left was just another desk with no chair, but that didn't catch Diana's eyes since they immediately darted back to the bookcases. Diana forcibly retracted her smile and walked a little further ahead.

"This is, of course, the library. It's not that large, but..."

"Not that large?!" Diana questioned, looking over to Charlemagne with her smile anew. "It's massive!"

Charlemagne looked at Diana with curiosity as he saw the girl smile for the first time. Diana tried to hide her expression as she turned her back to Charlemagne and went ahead to some of the books in the middle aisle.

"Some of the books are manuals in the various fields of research I've managed to purchase, and some of them are my own journals half-filled with some of my own research. I doubt you'd find anything interesting there..." Charlemagne insisted as Diana began to examine some of the books.

"*Edwin's Guide to Advanced Biology*... a blank book with nothing in it... oh! Here we go! *Alice in Wonderland* – but I've already read that one," Diana said to herself with glee. "You've really got to get an organization system here, old man," she said to Charlemagne, still standing at the doorway. "A library this big couldn't nor shouldn't be this empty and messy – not to mention the manor. What gives, old timer? Why's this place so decrepit?"

"It's under stasis," Charlemagne explained. "I'm, uh... well, I was (before you showed up) planning to move. I sold off most of the furniture and décor. I kept and stored what was irreplaceable and valuable. I threw out what didn't sell and was meaningless (not to say it wasn't all meaningless). A lot of the books were donated in that process..."

"Where?"

"I'm not sure... charities? Schools?"

"No, I mean where were you going to move to?" Diana clarified. "A bigger mansion?"

Charlemagne didn't respond. Instead, he crossed his arms and looked at Diana as she continued to entertain herself with the books.

"This place must have been beautiful with the shelves filled! I bet you used to have a bunch of wonderful books too!" Diana remarked as if she was talking to herself as Charlemagne looked out the window, paying little attention. "Are there more bookshelves upstairs?"

Diana stood up and rushed over to the spiral staircase to find more (empty) bookcases backed against the same wall with a door at the left end.

"I hardly thought I'd take you for a book worm," Charlemagne cynically commented.

Diana's smile dropped as she looked down and held a hand on the railing. She moved her hair behind her. She avoided to reply and instead went back downstairs to the periodicals and academic magazines that she did find in pursuit for something to read.

"Well, I can see the tour is over," Charlemagne said, pushing himself away from the door frame he stood under. "If you need me, I'll be in my study."

Diana was left alone in the silence of the library with the rain and the books to keep her company.

"What an asshole," Diana murmured to herself, reflecting on the mild insult Charlemagne had landed on her.

Diana got up from where she was knelt as she held a copy of *Frankenstein* by Mary Shelley in her grip. She walked over to the tall, wide window and opened its curtains to expose the rest of the front lawn and the light offered by the outside. She could see the front gates from the driveway and road ahead, looking as far as the river over the cliff. She turned around with the book still in hand and walked over to one of the brown sofas to sit down, open the book, and try and find where she had left off back in Harlech when he had his own copy.

•

"Dear Richard," Charlemagne said to himself as he typed into his computer. "I'm sorry for failing to arrive in Harlech for the negotiations. Please extend my apologies to all our dear guests that arrived and missed my presence. Unfortunately, I have a bit of a problem back home..."

Charlemagne jerked his eyes away from the computer screen as the study door opened with Diana gently walking inside.

"Don't you know how to knock!" Charlemagne snapped over to Diana as she stood in the corner of the room.

"Calm down, grandpa," Diana replied with a neutral expression. "I just came to tell you that dinner is on the way..."

"Dinner?" Charlemagne questioned. "We *just* ate!"

"Yeah, like... four hours ago. It's almost six o'clock now, and I'm hungry."

"Fine," Charlemagne admitted, looking over to the grandfather clock next to the fireplace on the opposite side of the room. "Is that all? Could you –"

"Whoa! Is that a model of King Island?!" Diana questioned, looking at the scale-model of the third island of Harlech in the middle of the room.

"Oh, for God's sake," Charlemagne muttered under his breath.

Charlemagne ignored him and continued to type.

"You've even got the Penultimate Bridge and all the districts exactly as they are..." she said, examining the suspension bridge over the Harlech River. "Camross... Whitney Harbor... King George Park... Central Harlech... Stoneridge... Bromley... the Industrial District – and even Keswick..."

Diana examined the last district she said carefully as her eyes searched and dilated at a particular building. She swallowed with a grim face before raising it up and looking to Charlemagne.

"Did you build this?"

"No," Charlemagne scoffed. "An architect in my company built it and brought it here for a meeting I had several weeks ago. Not that the meeting mattered seeing that the company is being liquidated... not that I *can* liquidate it seeing that I am grounded here!"

"Dude, why don't you just video chat those meetings?" Diana remarked. "It isn't the dark ages."

"These aren't any ordinary meetings!" Charlemagne snapped at her, standing from his desk. "These are negotiations to sell one of the oldest and largest companies in the world! My presence is the most mandatory of them all – not to mention the impression I need to maintain in these last moments..."

"Fine, if you say so..." Diana replied. "Why sell the company though? Doesn't it have your name?"

"It's more complicated than that..." Charlemagne explained. "Cabernet Industries is a conglomerate, meaning, it is an enterprise that owns a variety of different branches, separate companies, divisions, brands, etcetera, such as Cabernet Extraction, Cabernet Forestry, or Cabernet Technology. The companies themselves aren't being sold off as much as their assets are. Why? Because I'm getting old and want to retire to be at peace. I don't need wealth. I don't need capital. I don't need you here to ruin my plans either!"

Charlemagne took a moment to catch himself as he cleared his throat from his outburst.

"I don't need the responsibility of a company with my name on it. All I want to do is to sell the mega-corporation to ensure no hands can at least corrupt the family name. This is nothing new to the members of the board and was expected to happen eventually. There are only three of us left in the Cabernet family and neither of us have any heirs to inherit what should have been passed on."

"So, you'll kill it then? One of the few honest companies to feed a bunch of megalomaniacal ones?"

"Did you not listen to what I said? Even then, are you so cynical? The companies on the partition table aren't 'evil.' They will do well with the assets they plan on purchasing. Take Obelisk Mills for example. They're a lumber company that is looking to pretty much take over Cabernet Forestry."

"Obelisk Mills? They're pretty much the definition of an 'evil' company as far as businesses go. Do you live under a rock? Haven't you seen the acres of deforested rainforest in the Amazon they've left behind? Or the statistics on deforested animals that have died because of deforestation by their hands?"

"You sound like a petty liberal," Charlemagne remarked, moving from the other side of the model to put his hand on the doorknob out of his office. "You haven't been in the industry – no less as long as I have. You don't understand the realm of business. Furthermore, Obelisk is a decent company with a decent name under a decent man. They're not the antagonists you perceive to see with these rumors and biased researchers. Either way..."

Charlemagne dropped his eyes to the floor before moving them back to Diana as the front door began to ring its obnoxious tune.

"I won't be changing my mind. I'd rather oversee the liquidation while I'm still alive than leave it to the attorneys when I'm dead... if I'll ever die at this rate. My God. The portions of the company will be divided and go to the highest bidders with the largest demand – it's as simple as that!"

With his final word, Charlemagne shut the door behind him and left to leave Diana in his study. She looked around the simple room with its brown carpet and coffee-brown wooden walls. The model of King Island stood in the center of the room to take up the most space, while a fireplace sat on the center-end closest to the door. Charlemagne's desk sat on the opposite-end. Two armchairs were on either side of the desk, pushed up against the wall with a fish tank next to the one on the right and a short-wide bookshelf on the left. The walls were plain without the decorations Diana could imagine. The desk itself had a mere computer set up with a legal pad, telephone with a blinking red light, and stationery scattered around.

Diana walked over to the desk and pulled out the rolling black chair to sit down. He looked at the blank computer screen and then over to the flashing light on the telephone. Compared to the other phone in the mansion, this one was wider with a variety of different buttons. She put her hand over the mouse of the computer and woke up the sleeping computer. Charlemagne hadn't signed or logged off. The screen displayed Charlemagne's emails. Diana began to scroll through until she clicked on an email from earlier today sent by a man named Richard Huxley. She opened a separate tab on the Internet browser, typed the man's name, and waited for search results to show a picture of a clean-shaven man in a suit and wide smile. He had light brown hair styled neatly atop the middle-aged businessman's head.

According to the search engine, Richard Huxley was the incumbent Chief Executive Officer and President of Cabernet Industries. Diana clicked back to the email and began to read. She then re-read the part that intrigued her the most. According to the email, the many divisions of the company were to be abolished once all assets were bid off after a series of negotiations which were meant to be held earlier this morning in Harlech. Obelisk Mills wasn't the only sinister company on the list. A Russian oil company called Petrolgrad was interested in obtaining the lease on oil fields, oil rigs, and refinery plants. Several American weapon companies such as DARPA were set to acquire Cabernet Technology. Several construction firms were eyeing Cabernet Construction.

"All these assets..." Diana quietly said to herself. "Divisions with their own divisions."

Diana closed the email and opened another tab to search Cabernet Extraction. She opened the first article and began to read about the many acres of land owned by the mining and oil company alongside the many manufacturing, refinery and steel mills under its same eye. She then opened another page to search Cabernet Forestry and learn about the many acres of Canadian land under its ownership for the purpose of 'disciplined' removal and regrowth.

Cabernet Industries was a company with a good reputation led by good people, but all these other companies were unlike it and wouldn't take the extra step to protect their valued image. These other companies weren't as old with a reputation as large as Cabernet. Diana relaxed her hand from the mouse and frowned at the thought of Charlemagne selling his company off for the sake of his own retirement. He was the most depressive person that she had ever meant, which said a lot given her upbringing in one of the most depressive locales in the entire country.

Diana moved her eyes over to the answering machine with its light still flickering. She moved her finger from the mouse to hit the play button.

"Your mailbox is almost full," a monotone male voice said. "You have ten new messages and fifty-five saved messages. First new message: May 7th at 12:56 PM."

"Hey, Charlemagne. It's Salmar again," a calm male voice said. "I'm not sure you got my first message, and I know you're busy, but I'm just calling again so we can meet up and talk about the issue with the company. Thanks."

The answering machine beeped.

"Second new message: May 9th at 10:06 AM."

"Come on, Charlie," the voice from the last message (Salmar) said. "You don't expect me to believe you're not getting my messages, do you? Call me before the meeting on the twentieth, will you? Thanks."

The answering machine beeped again at the end of the message.

"Third new message: May 10th at 9:31 PM."

"Charles," Salmar said in a sterner tone, "what's going on? I came by the manor and not a car was in sight. The place looked like a tomb from the windows. I tried calling the penthouse, but Allodia said you weren't there. She hasn't seen you either. Call me, will you? Do *not* sell Cabernet Industries."

The answering machine beeped again.

"Fourth new message: May 12th at 2:56 PM."

"Okay, I know you're still in town. I called Richard and he said that he saw you earlier this morning. He also told me that you seemed serious and emotionless. I'm worried about you, Charles. We all are. Call me, please. We don't have to talk about the issue with the company... okay, maybe we do, because it's clearly a symptom of this clear depression. Anyways, please call me as soon as possible please."

The answering machine beeped again.

"Fifth new message: May 15th at 11:16 AM."

"Charles, it's me, Richard," a new, deeper voice said. "I just got off the phone with Saul Bagman from Lovegood Pharmaceuticals and they've agreed to our proposal (finally)."

Richard sighed over the phone.

"I'll let you know what the reps from Maikuro Incorporated say about their portion of Cabernet Electronics. It might all just go to Lang Innovation. Anyways, I just wanted to give this quick update. I've got to go."

Diana continued to listen attentively. She felt struck by the talk of the company being sold off as though she was a jealous girlfriend. She was also curious to know why Charlemagne was avoiding calls from this Salmar character. Halfway through the sixth message, Diana grew bored and skipped it. She skipped all the messages up to one from yesterday.

"Ninth new message: yesterday at 10:40 PM."

"Okay, the deal is going off tomorrow, but please, hear me," Salmar said. "Think about our parents. And then think about Dad's parents. Cabernet Industries has its foundations in legacies built generation after generation, and it's not fair that you get to derail all of that just because you're the eldest! Cancel the meeting, please!" Salmar paused for a moment before returning with a calmer voice, "Let me talk to you as soon as you can. Allodia wants to talk to you too. Goodbye."

The answering machine beeped one last time.

"Tenth new message: today at 03:20 PM."

"Charles, it's me again," Salmar said with an anxious, but happier tone. "Is everything okay? Allodia and I sat like idiots in the boardroom waiting for you to show up at the tower. I'm going to hope that you not showing up means that you've changed your mind. Listen, I just got back from Harlech about an hour ago, and I have to go pick up my son from soccer practice. Yeah, I've got a son, I know. An adopted one, albeit, but hey.... You'd have known that had you not been as reclusive as you've been. Anyways, I'm negging you. I'm just happy that you've decided to change your mind, but still wish you'd talk to me and sis. Talk to you soon (hopefully)."

"End of message. You have no new messages. Sunday, May 21st at 07:45 PM."

Diana sat in Charlemagne's chair for a moment to think before standing up. She thought about this Salmar character. If there was anybody to help her try and stop the selling of this company then perhaps he could. Diana left the study immediately before Charlemagne found her still here. She went straight to the kitchen to meet up with Charlemagne for dinner.

Act 1, Scene 4

The next morning, Charlemagne sat in his office chair in his study, looking at the computer screen. He had tired eyes and a cup of coffee next to his keyboard.

"Oh, good Lord. What's this?" Charlemagne muttered under his breath upon reading an email from Richard.

Charlemagne gave a sigh and closed the message before finding a new one from B.C. Child Services. He clicked on the email from the social worker that saw him yesterday. Mr. Macintyre had somehow managed to get his personal email. He had sent Charlemagne an email with information about Diana. Charlemagne scrolled through the letter in disgust as he scoffed.

According to the email, the girl was enrolled at the only nearby high school: Lord Phoenix Secondary.

"What day is it?" Charlemagne questioned himself, perking up in his chair.

Charlemagne looked over to his answering machine and checked the date to be the 22nd of May.

"Is that a Sunday, Monday, or what?" Charlemagne said before opening the calendar on his computer.

"Monday," he confirmed. "Good Lord, I haven't even heard from the brat. Did she go to school? I better check to make sure."

Charlemagne stood up and began to dial the school number as he read it off the computer screen. He took the wired telephone in hand and put his free hand in his pocket as he walked to the other side of his desk. Charlemagne looked ahead as the phone rang and through the windows on each side of the fireplace to get a good look outside to where he could see Diana sneaking around from the trophy room. Charlemagne immediately hung up as he slammed the phone down on the answering machine. He then rushed across his office to get a better look out the window.

"If the lass was trying to look suspicious, then she was doing a fine a job of it," Charlemagne said, watching her as she looked around.

Diana walked over to the stairs in the garden, stepped down, and went out of sight to Charlemagne's view. He stepped back and went back to his computer. He opened up the software belonging to his security cameras throughout the property. He then quickly opened the feed of the perimeter of the mansion.

"Truancy. She should be at school. Where has she gone?" Charlemagne questioned as he checked several cameras in the gardens. "Oh, there she is."

Charlemagne looked closely at his screen as he watched the girl sneak through the empty horse pen and avoided trying to step into the mud. The girl stopped at the large barn doors going into the garage. She began to produce something from her denim jacket.

"What the hell is she up to?" Charlemagne muttered to himself as the girl put something between her lips. "Oh, for God's sake!"

Charlemagne got up from his desk and marched out of his study. He immediately went through the library and outside hall to quickly pass through the grand foyer and made it into the opposite wing. He then went ahead through the kitchen, into the storage closest, and into the attic above the garage before climbing down a ladder to step on the stone floor of the garage. Charlemagne walked past the empty horse stables and those renovated to store the various vehicles kept on the property. He then went forward and avoided opening the large garage doors for a thinner, normal one besides it on the left. He opened it, went through, and raised his eyes over to Diana as she was smoking with her side against the barn exterior wall.

"Oh, sh–!"

"What do you think you're doing?!" Charlemagne questioned as he walked into some mud. "Oh, you see! I've soiled my shoes now because of you!"

"Tough," Diana remarked.

"These are Italian leather!" Charlemagne complained, annoyed at her before grabbing the cigarette out of Diana's hands. "Where did you get this?! Where did you even learn to smoke?"

"On the streets I was born on, old man," Diana replied, reaching for the cigarette as Charlemagne raised it to tap the bud on the wet exterior walls of the barn. "Hey!"

"You're merely, what? Twelve years old? How could you be starting an addiction so early? Do you want to die? Death is what you'll get if you smoke, but not so mercifully either – not before losing your voice, having your kidneys fail, throat choke up and being doomed to some sort of malignant cancer and whatever malaise that adds along. How could you throw your youth away like this? My, if I were you-"

"Oh, shut up," Diana complained. "What's it to you? I'm fourteen and I can do whatever I want! Who are you? A doctor? What do you even care if I die – it's my life! Death is better than this crap I'm going through now!"

"Do not be so naïve or ungrateful about your youth. You're in a better situation than me. And no, I'm not a doctor, but a scientist," Charlemagne replied. "That and an assortment of other things, but I'm trying to retire no thanks to you. That doesn't matter though. I'm taking you to school."

"School? I don't go to school," Diana complained.

"You do now," Charlemagne replied, grabbing Diana by the arm and dragging her inside.

"Get your hand off of me!" Diana cried out. "Why do you have such a strong grip?" she added as she tried to get free. "I don't need school! I learned everything I need to know already!"

The two of them froze in the middle of the garage as Charlemagne let go of Diana. He gave her a nasty glare.

"Clearly, seeing as you've learned the right habit," Charlemagne remarked, showing his hand to Diana. "Give me the cigarettes."

"I'm not giving you my smokes," she bitterly replied.

Charlemagne retracted his hand. He grabbed the girl by her wrist and with the other took the package from her denim vest to put in his blazer pocket.

"Look, I can imagine if the public system in Harlech is a little *laissez*, but it's different here. If you don't show up, then the police show up at your doorstep. I do not need public attention called to me by dragging a twelve-year old girl out of my house, so please, try and cooperate. It's them or me. Who do you want to take you to school?"

The two glared at each other and Diana didn't reply. She stood her ground.

Act 2, Scene 1

Diana sat in the police cruiser, arms crossed as she was dragged across town. She was quiet and turned her gaze into the window next to her as they pulled up to a small two-story building with a large three-story annex joining on the right.

"Here we are, kid," the officer said in his rustic accent. "What class do you got?"

"I don't know," Diana replied with a shrug. "I'm new here, I guess. I've never seen this place in my life."

"You guess?"

"I was dragged here from my home in Harlech to live with that Cabernet creep. I don't want to be here!"

"Aw jeez..." the officer sighed, getting out of the driver's seat to go around and let Diana out. "Cabernet told me that you're his adopted daughter. You can't just skip school, ma'am. Come on," he added, opening the door for her. "I'll take you to the office so they can get you sorted out."

Diana moved herself out of the car and stepped onto the sidewalk. She looked at the school ahead and gave a distasteful moan. The school was a two-story brick building with large, black-framed windows spread about. Together, the officer and Diana walked up the front steps into the building to come into the main hallway. The building was as old inside as it was on the outside. Inside it had a white-tiled ceiling and plain white laminate floor. The surrounding walls were salmon pink with dents and scratches if not tall grey lockers in groups.

The officer led Diana to the immediate right where they entered a warmer room with black chairs on the left and a long counter across the left. It also had a clean brown carpet.

"Officer?" an older woman greeted from a desk ahead.

On the far-side of the office were cubicles. One of the cubicles towards the right was occupied by this older woman. She looked to be in her sixties at most and late fifties at least. Her greying hair was untidy despite the bun it was tied in. Her clothing was elegant, but also casual. She wore a pink turtleneck sweater with a golden chain necklace and Christian cross. She had a brooch on her right breast. She also wore black trousers and loafers. Her main feature was her thick-rimmed glasses over her old eyes.

"I've got a drop-off for you," the officer said. "Straight from Cabernet Manor too – Mr. Cabernet said that she's a foster child staying with him, and that she'll be new to this school."

"Oh, is that right?" the woman replied, looking to Diana. "And you are?"

"Diana..." she replied, with a disgruntled look and while clenching her teeth.

"I'm sorry, dear?" the woman asked in a louder voice.

"Diana Cambridge," she repeated a bit louder, but more annoyed and with more bitterness.

"Oh, I see," the woman replied, searching through a binder ahead of her. "Hm, we've got no records on you... but of course. There's a sticky note here from Glenda. Don't worry, officer. I can take it from here. The principal will be seeing Ms. Cambridge no doubt."

"No problem," the officer replied. "Always a pleasure. Can I get your name, love?"

The officer took out a notebook from his belt and produced a pen.

"Meredith," she replied. "Last name: McKinnon."

"Thanks, love," the officer replied upon writing the name. "Take care."

The officer turned around and left the office. Diana remained where she stood.

"Just wait a moment here while I go see if Mrs. Phillips is busy," Meredith said, standing up and rushing over to a door on her left.

Meredith started to knock and soon after, the door opened to present a short woman (taller than Diana). She had dark brown hair, wore a pinstripe black blazer, and had a matching skirt and stilettos. She had pale skin, and her hair was long. She looked a little like Morticia Addams if her lipstick was only black (it was pink).

"Yes, Meredith?" the woman asked from around the door in a soft voice.

The old woman, Meredith, started to quietly talk to the principal. Diana raised an eyebrow over as she tried to listen in with curiosity, but she couldn't catch a single word. Instead, the door widened and the two women looked over to her.

"Hello, Diana. My name is Principal Phillips," the woman said to him in a kind voice. "Come and have a seat in my office. I'll get you to your first class as soon as I can."

Diana stood up and walked over to Mrs. Phillips with hesitant steps. She gave Meredith a displeasing glare as she passed her. Diana entered the office and Mrs. Phillips closed the door behind her before walking over to her desk. The two of them sat down in the small room where there were many books scattered around and an old wooden desk in the middle. Plain blue armchairs were ahead for Diana to choose between the two, while Mrs. Phillips had her black office chair.

"How are you, Diana? We have lots to discuss," Mrs. Phillips said.

"Such as why I'm late?" Diana questioned with an aggressive tone.

"No, nothing like that, dear," Phillips assured her. "Although, please remember for future reference that classes start at a quarter to nine in the mornings."

Diana looked at her with a displeased face – a similar one that she's held in the manor since her diaspora from Harlech.

"Instead, I have to talk about your transfer from British Columbia. I have all of your records from the B.C. Ministry of Education.... It says here you never graduated from elementary school, nor did you take your Foundation Skills Assessment in Grade Seven. Although, I have your FSA from Grade Four and an interim report card from Grade Five. The paper trail stops right about there. You didn't complete any grades ahead of the fourth. Why is that, if I may ask?"

"Family," Diana replied.

"Right," Mrs. Phillips responded, biting her lip. "Hm, well, seeing as it is still early into your academics, I suppose I can just bump up to the ninth grade so that you'll be in classes with peers your age. It wouldn't be fair to hold you back – unless you had some sort of objection to that."

"I don't care. I'm not going to be here long."

"Oh, and why's that?"

"Because I never last long in any home I go," Diana replied with seriousness.

Mrs. Phillips nodded at her response before asking, "Who is your guardian at this moment? I was told that a police officer had to bring you in. I wasn't informed of who you are with. Is it a parent? Family?"

"I don't know," Diana remarked with a stubborn tone as she folded her arms.

Phillips leaned back and began to tap a pen on her desk in frustration.

"Okay then," Mrs. Phillips quietly said to Diana, moving some papers around on her desk and looking at a single sheet before turning it around to show her.

"I'll need to contact your guardian. In the meantime, I think it's time we got you to class so you can get to know your peers. This is your timetable," she added, handing her the paper in her hands. "I noticed that you didn't seem to have anything with you. No backpack. No books. No pens or pencils."

"Nope."

"Well, this is curious," Mrs. Phillips said, crossing her arms as well. "It's nearly time to break for the summer and you'll just be joining class now that we're so close to final exams. I'll have to see about some remedial education this summer to ensure you're ready for tenth grade. There is one provincial exam that you'll need to take at the end of it – an exam which students are supposed to take at the end of Grade Nine. I'll schedule you to take it in August."

"You've got to be kidding me," Diana refuted. "Don't bother."

"I'm afraid so, Diana. We'll do our best to try and accommodate you into your intended grade, but in order to ensure you perform to your best ability, we're going to have to crackdown on the basics you've missed."

"Basics? Oh please, what's so important in science or history that I've missed and will need to know for the coming year?"

"Lots, Ms. Cambridge. For example, how to write a properly structured paragraph, or an essay. There's how to prepare a scientific lab report according to the scientific method. History? You need to know the proper ways to interpret history, to look for bias, and consider differing points-of-view. You need to know the difference between primary and secondary sources. How history cannot always be an authentic representation of the past, but instead our interpretation based on evidence available. There is lot that the lower grades prepare you for, and I fear that it'll be quite a jump from fourth to tenth – especially in math. This is six years of gradual intensification you've missed out on.

Mrs. Phillips paused for a moment as she looked at a folder on her desk. She opened it and read a label atop.

"Ah, here's your address... only that's... curious."

"What is?" Diana asked.

"2316 Cliffside Way. I didn't think there were any houses along there besides the mansion."

Diana didn't respond.

"Is that the Cabernet home? Do you live in the old manor by the river?"

"Unfortunately," Diana replied with disgust.

"I'd have thought this to be a mistake, but here's all the proof I need. Charlemagne de la Cabernet is your current guardian. I guess I've learned something new... are you family?"

Diana tensed her crossed arms and shook her head.

"Not to that old coot," Diana protested.

"Now there, there's no reason to be so disrespectful to Charlemagne. Tisk, tisk. How irresponsible of him, however. Very irresponsible of Charlemagne to have a policeman drop you off as opposed to himself. I'll enjoy phoning him later in the day."

"Yes, *very* irresponsible of him," Diana replied with a fiendish smile. "He's a terrible guardian and has neglected me since I got to his home. I had to call the police myself after he *refused* to drive me here," she lied. "I had no other way of getting here. I didn't even know where here is!"

"I'm so sorry to hear that..." Mrs. Phillips replied with empathy, "but why would Charles adopt? He honestly hasn't changed a bit, has he? He has not ceased to surprise anybody with his next impulsive decision."

"I don't know," Diana shrugged, turning her face away. "Publicity? Then again, he seemed pretty clueless about this, so I don't know... but I have another theory."

"Charles—I mean, Mr. Cabernet, was never interested in publicity. He's always downplayed the newspapers and talked to my husband, the police chief, loads of times when it came to getting the press off his back, especially when it came to little incidents that could be blown out of proportion."

"Incidents?" Diana questioned with a little worry.

"Yes, incidents. Charlemagne is known in this town as an eccentric scientist – an adventurer and neo-explorer – an inventor, or innovator. He's been quiet in the last couple of years, but when he was younger, he used to be much more rampant."

"Doing what?"

"Oh, you'll have to ask him. I've said too much already. It's not fair nor nice to gossip. Come now, it's time you went to your first –"

The sound of a loud bell started to go off just as Mrs. Phillips was about to finish her sentence.

"Well, I suppose your second class now. I'll write you a note for... Mr. Hughes, and send you his way," Phillips said, drawing out a legal notepad and scribbling in cursive with the same pen she's retained in hand.

Diana took the note once it was ripped out of the notepad and handed to her. With both the schedule and said note in hand, she stood up with Mrs. Phillips. The principal extended a hand to her for a handshake.

"I'll talk to your other teachers," Mrs. Phillips said as Diana reached over to shake her hand. "Until then, we'll be in touch."

Diana looked over to her from the door one last time before nervously nodding to her. She closed her door behind her after she walked out, glanced to Meredith as she typed on a typewriter, and left the office.

"A typewriter…" Diana muttered. "A typewriter – in this day and age."

Upon leaving the office, Diana found herself in a thin crowd of unfamiliar teenagers. The anxiety in her stomach soared as she froze for a moment at all the people, some of which looked back at her. She looked around for a moment before swallowing her fears.

Diana stepped forward with the two pieces of paper in hand as she tried to avoid making eye contact with anyone, if possible. She felt anxious enough about not having a backpack or items that she should have. She went towards a set of stairs at the end of the main hall and came up to an identical large hall on the second floor. Diana had guessed her second period class to be on the second floor by the fact that it was in Room 204. She went ahead and came to the second classroom on the left where she found a room where some students (people her age) were walking into. Diana froze outside of the classroom as she hesitated to go inside. She could see an adult at the front of the classroom, sitting in a large wooden desk and poking into a plastic container with his lunch in it.

The teacher was middle-aged with glasses, dress pants, and a collared shirt. He had tanned skin and hunched over his desk as he ate the salad he had brought to work with him. A couple more students walked into the classroom before Diana stepped forward with her schedule and note in hand. She made her way towards the teacher, walking faster after he had turned to her.

"Hi," the man said, giving his attention to Diana.

"Hello," Diana awkwardly and quietly said to the man before handing the note as though she was a courier.

"What's this?" the man questioned, taking the note and opening it as he wiped his mouth with a napkin.

The man read the note before lowering it and looking at Diana.

"A new student in May? Sure, why not…"

The man unfolded the note and placed it on his desk. He then turned back to Diana as she tried to step back.

"I'm Mr. Hughes, Diana" the man said. "I'll have a word with Mrs. Phillips later on about getting you to speed later, but for now, why don't you grab a seat in the back there?"

"Okay," Diana replied, giving a sigh of relief.

Diana went and did exactly that. She sat down and turned her head to the side to look out the window, which looked out into a hall adjacent, which itself had windows looking into a large room on the ground floor. Diana looked for a moment at her peers as she tried to stir confidence in getting to know their appearance. It didn't work. She turned her head back out the window as she waited for the bell.

Once the bell went off, Mr. Hughes rose from his chair and clapped his hand. Diana looked at him attentively as she kept one sleeve of her arm close to her face nervously, almost trying to hide herself.

"Good morning, everyone. Let's get started!" he said, walking over to the door. "We've got lots to cover today, but foremost, we have a new student with us!"

All the eyes in the room immediately turned to Diana as Hughes pointed to her. Her stomach flipped and she lowered her arm and laid both on her desk.

"Everyone, say 'Hello' to our new friend, Diana," Hughes said.

Diana heard a faint voice say hello, but she couldn't see who it was. Everybody continued to look at her before they turned back to facing wherever their attention was earlier.

"Excellent," Hughes replied to the 'enthusiasm' of his class. "Now then, let's get back to it."

Diana sank in her chair as the teacher started to instruct. She looked at the others with their binders and pens in hand, while she was empty-handed with nothing but a schedule in front of her. She sulked as the first minute went by, and then another as she came to realize that all of this was truly a fresh hell to add to her pain.

Act 2, Scene 2

Charlemagne climbed the steps of the left staircase of the foyer, reached the top, and went through and into the library balcony. He entered another door on the immediate right, crossed the corridor and came into the master bedroom of the house on the right. He then took his keys from the dresser on his left, found his blazer in the closet and put it on. Charlemagne then went back downstairs and rushed through the front door, down the three-steps to the driveway, and to his car just as the gates to the manor opened and a blue convertible pulled in to park behind him.

Inside the convertible was a middle-aged man in a pressed brown suit with combed back long blonde hair that went to his neck. Charlemagne froze as the man looked over to him with a serious face. He pulled up the parking brake and quickly hopped out of his vehicle while Charlemagne stepped back to turn around and go back inside. Charlemagne fumbled with the keys in his desperation to re-enter the house before dropping them.

"Charles!" the man shouted in an accent similar to Diana.

"Go away!" Charlemagne yelled back as he picked up the keys.

"Charles, come on now," the man said as he walked up the steps to catch up with him.

"I don't want to talk, Sal. I'm fine," Charlemagne argued, quickly unlocking the door and then opening it.

"Don't be like that! Why did you blow off the negotiations? You had sis and me worried!" Salmar argued as Charlemagne slipped behind the door and tried to close it.

Salmar lunged forward to shoot his foot between the door to keep it from shutting.

"I don't want to hear it," Charlemagne argued, slamming the door on his brother's foot.

The two of them looked down at each other's feet as Charlemagne continued to slam the door to get him to withdraw.

"Why are your shoes so dirty?" Salmar asked.

"It's a long, complicated and bothersome story," Charlemagne simply replied. "Probably has something to do with you, if you ask me, but I'll have none of it. None of it, I say!"

Charlemagne attempted to kick his brother's foot out of the way, but slipped his grip for Salmar to bust in.

"Oh damn!"

"We need to talk," Salmar asserted as he walked into his old childhood home.

"There's nothing to talk about," Charlemagne bitterly replied.

"Nothing to talk about?"

"I need to go into town. Can't this wait?"

"So you can ditch me again? I don't think so," Salmar replied, closing the door behind him before looking to Charlemagne. "Why've you been ducking my calls? What's going on with you?"

"I don't need to hear anything from you, Sal. Let me go before I call the police!"

"You don't need to hear it, but you'll hear it anyway. It's for your own good."

"Oh please, when did you ever care about Cabernet Industries? Where was this interest in the affairs of our family's legacy when you sold half of your share of the company to me so you could travel the world? Now that the company is what it is – now you're interested because you're scared that your inheritance will scatter away, aren't you? Admit it!"

"Charles…" Salmar replied, shrugging. "It isn't like that. I care about you. This isn't about the company. The company is not the issue here… you're the issue – the cause behind this effect. I'm here to talk about you and you alone. I'm surprised and thankful that I'm even looking at you right now, because God was I scared all of yesterday, especially when you didn't show. What's gotten into you? Where've you been? First you disappear for a year and nobody sees you, and next you're back in Harlech with an announcement to liquidate the company."

"I, uh… I did some light travelling," Charlemagne argued to the second question, crossing his arms impatiently before turning around.

"Light travelling?" Salmar questioned. "You were gone thirteen months and fifteen days according to Richard – with no contact to the outside world, may I add. You made Allodia the acting-chairman of the company after you came to the penthouse in the middle of the night, hounding on her door, and then ranting about how you needed to 'figure stuff out.' She was terrified. We all were."

"Happens to us all," Charlemagne remarked, shrugging.

"No, it doesn't," Salmar replied. "Even I wasn't like this when Gloria died."

"You're wasting your time, Sal. I'm calling the police," Charlemagne said, walking over to the telephone.

"Wait just a moment," Salmar responded, raising his hands up slightly. "Let me speak in some terms that you might relate to. Our great, great-grandfather built Cabernet Industries from the wineries they were in Lennox. He alone took that company forward with his contributions that diversified our market into resource extraction, resource refinery, construction, and manufacturing during the Laurier Boom. Our great-grandfather protected Cabernet during the Great Depression. Your hero, our grandfather, turned us into a world-renowned family with his own adventures and discoveries and pushed us from being the local 'Cabernet Corporation' to the multinational 'Cabernet Industries.' *Even* our own dad did his share with the Cabernet Foundation despite his hatred for it. Our father who never killed the company off and buried it – he could have, but no, he understood that the company wasn't his to destroy the same way it isn't yours. He waited until you were old enough to take control. Between the three of us, you always had more interest in it, and you made that clear when you founded Cabernet Tech and launched us into the current era. You may have nursed the company into what it is now, but that doesn't give you the *damn* right to abolish it all. It is *ours* and not just yours, because we're all Cabernet."

Salmar stopped for a moment as he thought. Charlemagne began to shake his head.

"Cabernet Industries… what it is now… it's a powerful thing, Charles. You can at least admit that having a majority shareholding is both powerful and dangerous (not that one company could cause an economic downturn), but that's not the point. It's dangerous because of what it could do to feed other companies, which together are more powerful and dangerous. Not to mention what it'll do to the economy – billions of dollars into foreign hands. I mean, are you crazy?"

"I'm very well and sane, thank you very much," Charlemagne replied, clenching a fist.

"Then *why* are you doing this?"

"Because I'm sick of it!" Charlemagne shouted, turning to him. "I've gotten to such a point where I have all the money in the world, and I have *nothing* to do with it. It's maddening!

I've dedicated my life to solving the unknown, learning all I can about the world, inventing new things, searching the cosmos, and done as much as I can... and for what? It... it feels like it didn't *mean* anything.... I... I don't understand *why* I wasted so much time doing all that, perhaps I was just selfish, and I liked it for my own gain, but now... I don't understand. It got so damn repetitive and cyclical... waking up in the morning, being shunned by my research department and every scholarly institution on the face of the world – doing everything myself and then falling asleep once I crashed from too much caffeine. I had enough of the lifestyle... I began to question *why* I was doing it and then it hit me... I had no reason or explanation that was worth the effort. There was no point. There's no point to anything! I could have kept going until I was an old man, but it wouldn't have mattered because down the line... only my discoveries and contributions would be remembered, but I... I'd be dead."

Salmar took a step back from his brother after his outburst. He took a deep breath as Charlemagne turned around again. Charlemagne put his hand on his forehead and began to rub it as he calmed down.

"And so, the rest of the family has to suffer because you're suffering? The lineage of the Cabernet family doesn't end with you, Charles. Hello! I'm here, Allodia is here. I have a kid! Cabernet Industries should at least belong to him!"

"This is what this is about," Charles said in a dark tone as he turned to face Salmar again. "You *do* want Cabernet Industries for yourself then. For your son..."

"Even if that *was* my reason, (not that it is, but) is that such a bad reason?" Salmar questioned.

Charlemagne shook his head before he started to shake. He moved away from the telephone and towards the hall going to the library.

"You had fifty years to figure all this stuff out, Charles," Salmar said, stopping him with his words. "I would have at least expected that my smartass brother could have at least figured out the purpose to life, but instead you're just a suicidal nihilist. How come you're questioning all of this now, huh?"

"I… I only did what felt right. I dropped out of university to pursue my dreams because it felt right. I… I never expected what I loved so much could eventually become boring, especially when I had been doing it for close to thirty years. I have nothing now, though. Nothing."

Salmar looked at his older brother apologetically. He walked over to him and put his hand on his shoulder in hopes of comforting him.

"You still have me. You still have Allodia," Salmar said. "Come on, let's go have a seat."

Salmar turned Charlemagne from the library and directed him towards the parlor.

"I'll make us some tea and we can talk about it all. I don't want to see my brother like this. Forget about the company for a moment and let's go sit down, relax, and just talk, okay?"

"No," Charlemagne passively resisted. "I… I have to go. I have to be somewhere…"

"No," Salmar replied. "You're not going anywhere until I feel like it. Come on, come and sit down and just calm down for a moment. Okay?"

Act 2, Scene 3

"Diana Cambridge to the office please. Diana Cambridge, to the office please. Thank you," the PA system of the school screeched.

Diana sat in her desk with a broken pencil she had found on the ground in one hand, and piece of paper in front of her that she had scavenged from a recycling bin. She rolled her eyes over the announcement and slammed the pencil down to stand up in the middle of her math class to leave. She had left behind all that she had.

The main hall on the ground floor was quiet. Diana slipped into the female washroom and walked towards the sink. She laid her hands around the rim of the porcelain sink and began to turn the tap on with one hand before looking up to herself in the mirror.

"Today has been the most miserable day of my life," she remarked to herself. "Did I survive on my own for this? To be ridiculed? To be embarrassed as I sat alone because Cabernet didn't bother to give me any money for lunch? Worst of all… to be the *new* kid with so many judgmental eyes looking at me…?"

Diana ran her right hand through the water and splashed some on her face to cool her stress. The adrenaline in her body caused her to tremble and stomach to never cease to relax. She looked at herself in the mirror one last time before turning the tap off. She then left the room, but instead of turning right to go down the hall and towards the main office, she instead turned left. Diana walked up and towards the staircase, turning right there to go down the rear hall.

Wide double doors were at the end of this side of the hall. Diana made her way towards them, peaked in one of the small square windows on either side and saw a bunch of kids in athletic gym strip standing around. She lowered her heels and thought to herself for a moment before looking to the door next to her with an exit sign above. Diana walked towards this door, looked through it, and saw a large soccer field behind the school. She fixed her attention especially at the bleachers on the far side of the field before opening the door and stepping out. She then walked casually across the concrete patio behind the school where there were some wooden picnic tables with closed parasols scattered around. Diana then stepped onto the grass and started to make her way across the field.

Diana arrived at the bleachers when she started to go around them. She stood behind the bleachers and found a metal pole. She then turned her back to it, slid down, and sat down in peace and quiet.

"As if the mansion wasn't bad enough… at least I actually had books there."

Diana began to take out the last cigarette she had in her pocket as she turned to her side and looked through the slits of the seats to notice the doors of the gym open up. A gym class began to make their way towards the field. Diana hit the back of her head into the pillar softly before rolling her eyes.

"Whatever," she muttered to herself as she brought out the lighter Cabernet failed to confiscate from her.

Diana flicked the lighter, put the cigarette between her lips, and started to try and light it. She struggled a bit due to a mild breeze that was coming in. She stood up and brought her hands together to shield the cigarette from the wind. It lit. Diana inhaled and then removed the cigarette with one hand while putting her lighter away with the other. She put the lighter into her jean pockets as a puff of smoke came out from her mouth like a huge sigh of relief. She leaned back into the metal pole and relaxed. The toxins settled in her lungs as she calmed.

"I don't want a new life..." Diana pleaded. "I'm just the same old girl. I don't need this. I want to go home..."

Diana raised the cigarette to her lips again for another intake, but flinched instead as a football made its impact beside her. She then turned forward with the appearance of a tall and fit lad who appeared and stopped before her. Diana struggled to react and looked around for someplace to bud out the cigarette, but it was too late. She simply held it in her right hand, between her fingers as the two looked at each other in silence for several seconds. Diana broke the silence with an aggressive frown, and...

"What are you looking at?" Diana challenged.

"Nothing," the boy responded with a slight rural accent.

The boy walked over to the football in a calm pace, picked it up and then looked back over to her. He had short and neatly trimmed strawberry-blonde hair and seemed to be about Diana's age. He had tanned fair skin from being outside too much, which complimented his hair color. He wore a white t-shirt, black shorts and black running shoes. His leg hairs stood out as they were golden all the way up from his thin ankles, to his calf muscles, and thighs underneath his shorts. He also had broad shoulders that stood out with his good posture. He looked away from Diana for a moment as he positioned himself to throw the football over the bleachers and back to the field.

After the boy launched it, he looked back at Diana with curiosity. He stepped over to her. Diana looked up from the boy's legs and looked at him.

"What do you think you're doing," the boy asked her with a frown on his face.

"Smoking," Diana simply replied, turning her gaze away from the boy and forwards instead.

"I can see that," the boy responded. "Where did you even get that or learn to smoke in this small-ass town?"

"In the city where I was born," Diana replied, annoyed and deliberately being obscure.

"You're what? In eighth grade?" the boy replied. "Shouldn't you be playing with dolls instead of cigarettes? Do you have a death wish or something? Trying to get lung cancer? Go ahead. It only gets worse as your life ticks away."

"I'm in ninth grade, you imprudent prick," Diana responded, straightening herself out as she stepped towards him. "Is everybody in this town a damn doctor?"

"Ninth grade? I doubt that. How come I haven't seen you around before?" the boy questioned. "I'm not a doctor though, but I hope to be one someday. Maybe I'll treat you for some sort of cancer when the day comes... if you make it that far."

The boy ran off with his last remark. Diana frowned at him and could only look at the stains of mud at the back of his legs and shoes. She scowled as the cigarette continued to burn in her fingers. It began to burn her fingers over the time she had been conversing with the boy. She flicked it onto the ground and smothered it with the sole of her right shoe. Diana then looked through the slits of the bleacher and targeted her eyes on the boy from earlier to see if he tattled on her. He was instead playing football happily with the other kids.

Diana kept her eyes on him for another minute before sighing to herself. She went around the bleachers and around the edge of the field to get back to the patio behind the school. She then snuck back inside and went to the main office.

Mrs. Phillips leaned over the main office counter as Diana entered.

"What's up?" Diana greeted as she looked over to her with surprise.

"Diana," she replied. "Where have you been? I paged you about thirty minutes ago…"

"I was in class," Diana replied with a sincere tone. "Mrs. Yaskova wouldn't let me go until now. Here I am."

"No matter," Mrs. Phillips replied, looking out the door into the hall as the final bell went off. "I got a hold of Mr. Cabernet about an hour ago, but he hasn't shown either. He told me he was on his way… he must have gotten caught up in something. That's quite alright though… do tell him to come tomorrow morning with you when he drops you off. Also, do remember to prepare for the day with the right supplies. It's not fair for you to have to suffer for his misjudgment and poor preparation."

Diana gave a light smirk as she mildly insulted Cabernet to her pleasure. The afterschool announcements began to project over them.

"That'll be all for today, Diana. Have a good afternoon," Mrs. Phillips said.

Diana nodded and left the office. She immediately turned left to head out of the school. A dozen cars were parked along the curb of the street ahead with patient parents waiting for their children. Diana looked around, thinking to see a luxurious black car or old man waiting for her, but shot the idea down as her mind filled with doubt. Instead, she sighed one last time and made her way down the steps of the school and towards the sidewalk. She tried to recall the path the police officer took this morning to get to the school so she could repeat it on foot.

The clouds in the sky turned darker with each step she took finding her way to the Nattau Bridge. Eventually, a crack of thunder filled her eardrums and echoed in her heart before it started to touch down with rain. Diana lowered her head in acceptance of her situation and continued to walk down the lone road with ranches, farms and acres of land on either side while she continued to walk to the mansion.

Act 2, Scene 4

The torrential rain hit the earth hard as the day turned into evening. Diana finally arrived at the mansion gates only to find herself locked out. She looked around the tall black metal gates of the driveway and began to think to herself as she shivered and felt a chill from her damp clothing. She continued to walk down the street to get to a shorter metal gate between the driveway gates with a path going up to the top of the driveway and front doors. She grabbed the bars to try and climb over. She set her foot on a rung of the gate, causing it to swing forward and open, letting her ride through.

Diana sighed to herself and jumped off. She then went up the stairs to the driveway and passed between the two cars parked atop. She glared at the black sedan and snubbed the blue convertible. Diana trudged forward to freeze at the three-steps up to the front door before looking up as a blonde man came out and closed the door behind him. He stopped to look down and over to her.

"Who are you?" Diana asked, stepping up.

"I should be asking you that," Salmar replied, watching Diana walk towards him and open the door.

"I'm the victim who's being kept here against my will," Diana remarked, entering inside and closing the door behind her.

Diana looked over to where she could see Charlemagne looking over to her from the parlor.

"Why are you soaking wet?" Charlemagne asked, walking over to her as she left a puddle at her feet.

"I'm wet because nobody was there to pick me up like all the other kids!" Diana replied with an angry tone. "I had to walk *all* the way back here using my memory alone because, like I said, *nobody* was *freaking* around to pick me up."

Diana walked past Charlemagne and went upstairs. Charlemagne didn't reply nor turn around. He simply stood in shock and embarrassment. Diana slammed the door behind her as she entered the antechamber outside the makeshift lab, which caused Charlemagne to snap out of his internal thoughts and walk after her with guilt.

Charlemagne came to her and knocked on the door. The door was left ajar and opened on its own. He looked inside and over to Diana as she searched her luggage frantically.

"What are you looking for?" Charlemagne asked.

"My other pack of smokes," she replied in frustration and anxiety. "Where are they?"

"I took them off you. You don't need them," Charlemagne replied, standing his ground. "Listen, I'm so-"

"Why did you take them!" Diana interrupted. "They were mine!"

"You don't need them!" Charlemagne argued. "If you're bored, read a book."

"It's not about boredom!" Diana remarked. "It's about stress! I *can't* read when I'm stressed!"

"You're fourteen. You shouldn't *be* stressed. What do you have to be stressed about?" Charlemagne questioned. "You don't have a mortgage. You don't have life commitments to uphold, or kids…. You've got yourself, and by the grace of God, a roof over your head…"

"And an incompetent idiot of a guardian who left me alone at a new school with *nothing*. An idiot of a guardian who forgot to meet with the principal – who forgot to give me lunch – who probably forgot I even existed until I got back!"

Charlemagne flinched over Diana's outburst and took a step back.

"I didn't ask for you to be brought here," Charlemagne refuted.

"I didn't ask to be brought here either!" Diana yelled, shoving her luggage aside so that she could sit down.

Charlemagne waited for a response, but Diana was silent as she simply trembled and brought her legs up. He continued to wait for a response, probably thought of something else to say to her to continue the argument but didn't. He instead stepped back and closed the door behind him instead. Charlemagne held his grip around the doorknob as he thought to himself. He then let go as he heard a sound come from the other side. Diana was crying.

Diana sobbed and sobbed as she fell over and simply cried in the ball she held herself in. Charlemagne stepped back from the door and walked down the hall with self-hatred. She didn't stop crying for at least five minutes when she finally calmed down. Diana wiped the tears from her cheeks and looked at the wet mark on her bed sheets from where she rested her face. She looked around the strange place and continued to cry as she sat up. Diana tilted her head down and rested her forehead on her knees to resume sobbing.

The tears came out stronger as she felt abandoned and imprisoned by this strange man. She felt like the loneliest woman in an alien world. She eventually fell over again as she choked in her sadness and tears.

Act 3, Scene 1

"You listen to me now," Charlemagne warned, waving his finger at Diana in the passenger seat next to him. "I don't want any mischief tonight. This is my brother's home, and I won't have you embarrass me."

"Sir, yes, sir," Diana replied with a mocking tone as she rested her head against the window beside her.

The two of them drove east, away from town and towards Salmar's home on the outskirts of the county. The headlights of Charlemagne's black sedan lit the way forward for them as they drove along the countryside road before coming off and onto a dirt road.

"The least I would like is to get through tonight as quickly and smoothly as possible. Am I clear?" Charlemagne reminded her.

Diana didn't bother to reply. She rolled her eyes. A month had passed since she was dropped off in this strange town and little had changed between the two. According to Charlemagne, Richard was working hard to keep buyer interest in Cabernet Industries, playing off the delay as a legal error. The legal error, to Diana, was her abduction to this town from Harlech. Mr. Gregson was still hard at work in figuring out a solution to this error. Meanwhile, Charlemagne worked on keeping his brother off his back as he compromised in having dinner with him at his home.

"Be glad that I'm at least dressed like this," Diana remarked, feeling uncomfortable in the black dress she wore for tonight's engagement.

"Oh, I am glad. I'm glad that you're in the least presentable as long as you don't corrupt a nasty image of yourself into my brother's mind. That dress is one of a kind. It came all the way from Paris."

"Yeah, I know. I saw the invoice. Seemed like a waste of money for just one dress. I could go my entire life in Harlech with that kind of money alone."

Charlemagne looked over to her and didn't respond as she made his way towards his brother's home. Salmar lived in a two-story farmhouse on the outskirts of town. It was a quaint home with a porch on the front. Diana noticed a black mountain bike parked in front of the porch. The house looked brand new in its construction through its appearance. It had gravel grey roof slates and a tanned flagstone foundation. The house was painted maroon and the rims of the windows were white. Charlemagne pulled up to the closed garage doors, shifted gears, pulled the parking brake and cut the engine before getting out. Diana got out on her side, stepped forward and looked over to see Charlemagne retrieving something from the back seats.

"Rich people..." Diana scoffed as Charlemagne picked up the wine he had brought with him from the cellar of the mansion.

The two of them made their way towards the porch, up the steps, and towards a front door. Charlemagne knocked on the door and held his breath with a wish that all could be over and done with so that he could go back home.

The door opened to reveal the combed-back blonde man that was Salmar de la Cabernet, the youngest brother of the youngest Cabernet generation. He was medium-sized in appearance as always, and Diana took notice in the contrasting figures of slim Charlemagne and fit, athletic Salmar. Salmar was dressed in black dress pants, a tanned brown dress shirt that was tucked in, a wine-red tie, and black suspenders. He held a smart phone in hand and had a wireless earpiece in his ear. He waved at Diana and Charlemagne before signaling for them to come inside.

"Hey, I've got to go. Yeah. Yeah, my brother just arrived with his kid. Yes, I know. Okay. I'll talk to you about it later," Salmar said before touching a button on his headset. "Sorry, that was just a client."

"Yes, yes," Charlemagne replied.

"Anyways, I'm glad you made it, Charles," Salmar remarked, taking his hand and shaking it. "How was the drive along? Did you get lost? Spook any wildlife this time, or did they spook you again?"

"Funny…" Charlemagne replied without laughter. "I had no trouble finding the place – I remembered the exact path from last time I was here, but I must say, I did not recognize the house as I drove in."

"Yeah, I had it renovated last autumn," Salmar replied with a light laugh, looking around the elegant, but simple foyer as he put a hand in his pocket. "Who's this lovely lady? Is this the kid you were telling me about?"

Salmar had looked down to Diana in her black dress. Diana had worked hard all day to create her current appearance. She had washed, brushed and done her black-brown hair so that it was wavy and side-swept. She also wore elegant black shoes to match her Parisian dress. She didn't wear makeup, and even if there were any in the mansion, she would have refused using any. She kept herself natural, authentic and minimal to please Charlemagne.

"Yes," Charlemagne replied for her. "Say 'Hello,' Diana."

"Hello," Diana plainly said in a negative tone.

"Well, aren't the two of you a lively bunch," Salmar remarked, turning to his left to lead them into the split living room, dining room, and kitchen.

The house was much warmer than Cabernet Manor with its lit incandescent bulbs and actual décor. The furniture was dusted and exposed unlike the covered furniture in the mansion, and there was an aroma of food cooking in the other room.

Diana looked at the foyer where a circular chandelier rested above, stairs were ahead on the right to go upstairs, and there were multiple directions to choose from. To the right was a sitting room, while forward appeared to lead to a hallway. The flooring consisted of white tiles and the walls were cappuccino brown. Diana followed the others to the right where they arrived into the next room.

The living room was closest to them. Diana looked over to the upholstered modern sofas, flat screen TV above a fireplace, and contemporary tanned carpet over the dark wooden floor under their feet. Behind the couch was the dining section with a rustic dining table and six chairs – two on each of the wider sides, and one each on the ends. Behind the dining section was the kitchen where a familiar-looking boy stood behind a counter, bent over and tapping into his smartphone.

"Ah, I almost forgot about this wine in my hands," Charlemagne remarked, presenting it to Salmar.

"Ah, yes. A little gift you've brought me…. Can I assume it's from the cellar in the mansion?"

"You can," Charlemagne replied.

"Very nice," Salmar nodded, taking it. "Uh…, Charles, this is my own adopted-son. His name is Tristan."

"Hi," Tristan replied, straightening up and putting his phone away.

"Yes, hello," Charlemagne replied.

Diana looked to him as she recognized him almost immediately. The red-blonde headed boy wore a light blue-collar shirt, unbuttoned at the top, but tucked into his beige dress pants he wore with a brown belt.

"Tristan, don't just stand there," Salmar remarked. "See that Diana is looked after and feels at home while I go fix my brother up a drink. It's time to crack this baby open…"

Salmar laughed as he looked to his brother.

"Come on, Charles."

Salmar walked forward, into the kitchen and into a room behind.

"Behave yourself and stick with this kid," Charlemagne whispered to her. "I'll be with my brother."

Diana looked at Charlemagne with a frown before looking back over to Tristan. Tristan was looking at the ground awkwardly as he anticipated being left with Diana alone. Charlemagne followed the path his brother took and disappeared into the back as Tristan smiled awkwardly at Diana. Once he was gone, he dropped his smile and frowned.

"Are you… uh, thirsty?" Tristan questioned, scratching his head as he looked away.

"I'm good," Diana replied, bringing a hand over the top of her forearm.

"Suit yourself," Tristan replied, shrugging and continuing to refuse looking at Diana.

Diana frowned at him before turning to the door the adults had disappeared behind. Salmar came back with two wine glasses in one hand and the wine bottle in the other. Salmar settled the bottle on the kitchen counter and put the wine glasses next to it.

"I hope nobody is hungry yet," Salmar said. "The roast only just went in not too long ago, so it'll be another while or so until it's ready. Tristan," he added, looking to him, "why don't you go show Diana your room. The adults need to speak in private, okay – keep your door open though, mister."

"Y-yes, sir," Tristan complied.

Tristan looked at both adults before walking between them. Salmar kept his eye on him as he approached Diana. Charlemagne stood weak in front of the refrigerator next to the door to the room behind the kitchen. Diana looked at Tristan as he walked over to him. He walked past her.

"Come on," he simply said.

Diana lowered her hand over her forearm, turned, and followed him. She looked to the adults one last time as Salmar began to pour the wine into each glass. Charlemagne looked at the glasses attentively. She turned her direction forward again and over to Tristan who was half-way upstairs already. She followed him.

Tristan entered his room, which was through the furthest on the right. His room was medium-sized with a single bed pushed in one corner, a window looking out west to the farmland beyond, a dresser, desk, and closet on each of the different sides of the room with the closet on the same side as the door. He walked to a corner of the dark room, looking out the window before turning around to look to Diana as she entered. She stood attentively at the door as she looked around.

"You, uh… can sit down," Tristan said. "Anywhere you want."

Diana didn't reply and instead nodded. She walked over to sit atop of his bed, near him. Tristan walked away to stand in the corner of his bedroom on the opposite side. He had his arms crossed.

"Before you ask," he said, causing Diana to look over to him as he looked to the side, "you can't smoke in here."

"Great," Diana simply responded, looking away from Tristan as he finally looked at her. "I wasn't planning on, but thanks for the heads up."

Diana focused her attention at the view Tristan had out his window. Tristan's eyes scanned Diana, which caused him to lower his hands and drop his frown.

"So... I guess you're the 'miracle' that Salmar was talking about, right?"

"I'm pretty sure it's 'curse' as his brother puts it instead," Diana replied.

"Which should I treat you as?"

"Take your pick," Diana sighed.

Tristan nodded without answering her. He stepped backwards and rested his back against the wall.

"Why do you smoke?" Tristan asked, not turning his attention away from Diana now.

Diana crossed her arms as she pulled herself backwards on Tristan's bed to sit more comfortably with her legs up and back against the window frame.

"Why do you care?" she questioned with an aggressive and annoyed tone.

"I want to know why you do it," Tristan clarified. "I'm curious."

"Well, it's not to be 'cool' like any poser might do it."

"Oh yeah? Is that so?" Tristan remarked, raising his eyebrows. "Why then?"

"Stress."

"What do you have to be stressed about?" he asked, sounding like Charlemagne.

Diana didn't reply to him. She instead snubbed him as she instead began to scan the room more thoroughly. Its décor was simple. It didn't have much of a personality or reveal much about the personality of Tristan.

Tristan thought to himself for a moment before he said, "I haven't been in this town for that long... since January really. I guess that makes two of us. I used to live with my parents in a town like this though. Salmar knew them... apparently, he worked with my dad before. He's a lawyer – Salmar, I mean – and took me up after they died. Now, he just does real estate thanks to the booming market around here, I guess."

"Your parents are dead?" Diana questioned, turning and facing Tristan. "I'm sorry to hear that."

The two looked at each other from either side of the room.

"It's alright, I guess. I... I don't think about it as much anymore," Tristan replied, tilting his head to the side. "What about you?"

"My father died years ago," Diana responded, looking down at the ground. "I didn't care much about him anyways. I hated him."

"What about your mom?"

"My mom... she died about two years ago," Diana replied with a sadder tone.

"I'm sorry to hear that," Tristan replied, looking over to Diana before he stepped forward to sit with her.

"Don't be," Diana responded without noticing Tristan next to her. "You have nothing to apologize for. I got over it as well."

"Brave," Tristan remarked with doubt in mind as he nodded.

Tristan stood up again. Diana noticed this. He walked over to his desk and sat down there instead. The two of them went into a period of silence between them. Diana began to grow feelings for Tristan – annoyance and bitterness as she grew tired with him.

"You, uh… do you like the town? The school?"

"Hell no," Diana replied. "I hate the school as much as I hate this damn town. It's hard to feel at home when everybody is so… empty and boring."

"Yeah…" Tristan smiled, laughing. "I grew up in a town like this, you know."

"You already told me that," Diana remarked.

"Oh… well, the town I grew up in was further up north in the province," Tristan said, lowering his smile with embarrassment. "Lord Phoenix is alright. I made lots of friends really quickly, which helped. Where are you from then?"

Diana looked over to him and said, "Harlech. It's a big city on the west coast. It's got about five hundred times the amount of people than this dump for the same surface area."

Tristan laughed at Diana and replied, "Yeah, I've heard of Harlech. It's hard not to. Salmar goes over there every once and a while for a special client."

"This Salmar guy… does he have a wife or something?"

"Nope," Tristan simply responded. "He's a widow. His gal died years ago and her grave is out back. I don't know much from that, and I don't ask about it either."

"Jesus, it's like death has followed everyone here," Diana remarked.

"Except Charles, I guess," Tristan replied.

"Hmm…" Diana thought without replying.

"Well, that's life I guess," Tristan said, shrugging.

The two of them went back into silence. Diana looked at Tristan as he scratched his head and looked down to his side.

"So, is there anything fun to do around here in this town?" Diana questioned.

Tristan shrugged.

"There's a theater in town. There's also an art gallery and then the river. There was an annual winter and spring festival, but the spring festival ended after Easter. Uh... I can't think of anything else unless you like being outdoors. Allabrese has a lot of that around itself."

"What about at home? What do *you* do for fun? I don't usually have much to do at my place, and this actually seems like a home than the manor..."

Tristan laughed again as he looked at Diana.

"You play sports?" Tristan asked, standing up and picking up a lacrosse stick near his closet. "Or, did you used to play any?"

"I used to play soccer in the alleyways with some of my neighbors, but that was ages ago. I didn't really have any place to go for sports, or to watch any. I'm a good runner though. I can run two miles in less than ten minutes."

"Running itself is hardly a sport though," Tristan replied with a smirk, putting his lacrosse stick down and standing before Diana. "Well, I don't have much in the way of entertainment in this place. I like spending my time outside the house when I can. I don't have anything fancy like video games. The TV is downstairs as well, and there's not much to watch on it. Salmar is a strict guardian. He wants me to focus on doing well in school. I could only barely convince him to buy me a phone after interim report cards so I could be in contact with my friends from school. I like to keep busy... I don't have much free time anyways."

"Salmar seems to be the opposite of my *caring* and *fantastic* guardian. Charlemagne doesn't give a crap about me.

The man is a killjoy and I'm pretty sure he's nuts. I don't know how he managed to adopt me or think he even did apply for me. He's such an arrogant and careless bastard."

"You've got a colorful mouth," Tristan remarked in his country-accent, crossing his arms.

"Aw, what's the matter? Why are you country folk so dense and polite?"

"It's not all of us. I was just raised in a Christian household. I'm Catholic."

"So? I'm Catholic too. I'm English by blood though – Cambridge – but you don't see me giving a *damn*."

Tristan sighed and rolled his eyes. The two of them stopped talking as they heard loud voices between the adults downstairs.

"Tristan!" Could you come downstairs, please?"

Tristan unfolded his arms and rolled his eyes. He left Diana behind as he left. She watched him leave her before he was out of sight, but not of mind. She thought about him as she looked out his window with a frown. However, he wasn't all that she thought about. She was startled moments later when she heard a creak of the floorboard behind her.

Tristan stood there and looked to her.

"Dinner's ready. Washroom is behind me for you to wash up… if that's something you do…"

Diana nodded, pushed herself forward from his bed, and stood up. She walked over to him and the two faced each other briefly. Tristan was about two or three inches taller than her. She walked past him and into the washroom to wash her hands. She felt Tristan's eyes looking at her as she washed her hands, closed the tap and dried them. The two then walked downstairs together for dinner.

After dinner had ended, the four of them continued to sit at the dining table without much to say. Diana looked between Salmar and Charlemagne at either side of the table. Each of them looked at each other in the same silence that Tristan and Diana had earlier upstairs. Tristan sat in front of Diana but was poking at his unfinished dinner.

"So," Charlemagne said, breaking the silence as he lowered his glass of wine, "how's work at the office going?"

"I'm not at the firm anymore," Salmar replied, sitting back in his chair with his hand around his glass of wine. "I run my own practice now. I primarily do real estate and business. I've been doing some work for one of the Cabernet competitors, Fitch Corp."

"Fitch Corp...." Charlemagne quietly replied with a tense body. "I think I've heard about them. They were in the news the other, I think."

"That's right," Salmar confirmed, raising his glass to take a drink. "I've been representing them as we try to manage old territories of their former owner."

"Jervis Fitcher..." Charlemagne recalled, "whatever happened to him? Pardon my ignorance, but I haven't been caught up with current events."

"A hostile takeover," Salmar quickly replied. "A suave young man rallied enough support for his own coup d'état against the company. I've heard things have been chaotic over the last quarter with stocks plunging, lay-offs being called, and the heat of stress being placed on the owner – some guy called Audric Zimmerman. He's the new majority owner and he's placed Harlech's own Mrs. Dulles as CEO to lead them out of the mud."

"Zimmerman... that name seems to ring some bells," Charlemagne said as he thought whilst stroking his chin. "Isn't there a Zimmerman on the board? I believe I met him when I was last in Harlech in April. Yes. He's new. How did he come into so much money to take over?"

"Well, between the coup, the revelation of Fitcher's tax evasion and near arrest that resulted in his suicide, it really wasn't hard. Especially when you consider that Zimmerman is a genius when it comes to the stock exchange. He was a stockbroker, and a *damn* good one too. He has his own company now... it's not even going to be called Fitch Corp anymore. He's giving it the name Zimmerman Corporation."

"Well, good for him," Charlemagne remarked. "It's a shame about Jervis though.... I believe I met his wife once – he had kids too."

"Yes, but he did have ties to the Harlech Syndicate," Salmar replied.

"But at least he had purpose... such a waste of life."

"Ironic of you to remark," Salmar remarked.

"Pardon me?" Charlemagne questioned.

"I said, 'Ironic of you to remark,'" Salmar clarified. "It's a little hypocritical that you're not okay that the scumbag killed himself *just* because he had a family. You have a family too, you know."

"Not entirely."

"Not entirely? Not entirely?! How ungrateful can you be, Charles?! My God! I've tried to be reasonable, but you're forcing me to come out and say it. You're a self-centered and selfish asshole. You don't give a damn about anyone, do you? No less do you care about the consequences of your own actions."

"Oh please. The vices are strongest in the critic. How many times have you been self-absorbed as well?"

"We're not talking about me, Charles. We're talking about you and the most impulsive thing you've come to do."

"Don't you mind what I do! I'm the chairman and majority-shareholder, and it's my final decision – a final decision of which, might I add, will go through whether you like it or not! The moment I can travel again, I'm going straight to Harlech and marching right to Cabernet Tower to sign every last deal on the table for every last bit of the company!"

"You bastard!" Salmar replied, slamming a fist into the table. "You have no idea what you're voluntarily allowing. Imagine the headlines! Imagine all the workers that will be laid off from the Cabernet family! Imagine these crooked international companies soar and profit from the downfall of the last good man in the room. You're not only dismantling our legacy, but you're smearing the name for all of us to be remembered as... as..."

"Oh, you really are a hypocrite, aren't you?" Charlemagne interrupted, standing from his seat. "You had your opportunity to make a namesake for the Cabernet family, but you refused."

Diana and Tristan looked at the two adults and sat in anxiety over the heated dispute. Salmar raised his hands up with his palms facing Charlemagne to usher some peace.

"I'm doing this for your own good, Charles, because I love you," Salmar remarked.

"No, Salmar, you don't," Charlemagne replied with a cold tone. "Goodbye."

Charlemagne ripped his napkin from his lap as it hung and was tucked inside his trousers. He threw it on the table and walked towards the foyer. Salmar stood up in protest and threw his wine glass towards the wall near the foyer.

"I'm this *close* to getting a damn insanity order on you!" Salmar yelled.

Charlemagne opened and slammed the door behind him.

"Fine, leave..." Salmar remarked, calming down again. "But you left your kid here!"

Diana was looking at Salmar as he said that. She moved back in her seat and started to get out to evade the awkwardness of sticking around. After an awkward pause in the silence, the front door opened again with Charlemagne poking his head in.

"Diana, we're leaving!"

The door then slammed shut again. Diana stood up and walked around Salmar to make her way to the foyer. She paused under the doorway between the foyer and living room.

"You better go, kid," Salmar said to her as she hesitated to leave.

The engine of the sedan outside started. Diana turned around and walked to Salmar.

"I want to help you," she said.

"I'm sorry, but there's nothing you can do to help. Just get to him before he gets angrier."

"He's not well. I've seen him every day for the last month, and there's something clearly wrong with him. What he wants to do with Cabernet Industries is a bad idea. It's not fair to let all these foreign buyers profit from (like you said) the last good man in the room."

Salmar looked at Diana but didn't immediately reply. He gave a single nod to her and walked into the kitchen. She stepped back into the living room as he opened a counter drawer and rummaged around. Diana looked over to Tristan as he awkwardly remained in his seat, hunched over and looking down. He took out an orange pill bottle and walked back over to her.

"Fine, kid," Salmar said as he handed the bottle to her.

The bottle had a white label across. It was prescribed to Salmar from a Dr. Schultz.

"Help my brother by getting these into him."

"What are they?" Diana questioned, taking the bottle and reading the label.

The label said they were 'citalopram.'

"They're, uh... candies to make Charles feel better – to make him feel happy enough to not sell the company – call them happy pills. We need to treat his major depression so we can stop what he's doing."

"I'm not five-years old," Diana replied, shaking the bottle. "I know what depression and anti-depressants are."

"Good. Give them to Charles once a day, every day until the bottle runs out. Ground them and hide it in his food. Do you think you can do that?"

"Yeah, of course," Diana replied, looking up to Salmar. "Did you... spike his food just now?"

"No," Salmar replied. "One dosage right now wouldn't have done much. These take time to really work – it's complicated chemistry. I didn't realize you'd offer to help, but had I known, I would have. Listen though, kid. If you can ensure he gets a pill every eight hours (twice a day) consistently, then he might start to feel better and think clearly."

"Right," Diana replied, looking at the bottle and then over to Salmar.

Diana turned to Tristan who was now leaning back in his chair with his arms crossed. He shook his head lightly. She then looked at Salmar once more before flinching and jerking her head over and out the window as the sound of the sedan honking viciously came from outside.

"Alright then, kid," Salmar replied, putting his hands on her shoulders to turn her around. "Do me proud and get going before he leaves you behind. The sooner you get that medication to him, the better."

"Sure thing," Diana said, stepping forward to brush Salmar's grip off. "I'll go."

Diana entered the foyer and looked at the bottle of pills one last time. She looked around for a place to hide them before she went outside, and decided to hide them inside her bra. Tristan watched as she opened the front door and then left. Diana walked down the porch steps, over to the sedan, and opened the passenger seat door to step in.

For the entire drive back to the mansion, she didn't even get a glance from Charlemagne due to the awkwardness in the argument. He was red with anger still and heat radiated from him all through the drive back. Once home, the car pulled in the manor driveway and Diana kept a hand over her chest to stabilize the bottle.

Charlemagne and Diana split paths when they entered the mansion. She went to her room and immediately took out the bottle from her bra to cusp with both hands once she was in the hall. She then brought it to the dresser to set atop. She looked at the bottle attentively and then stepped back to get dressed for bed.

Act 3, Scene 2

"This is your package for catching up on science," Meredith said, putting down a thick coil-bound book on the office counter between Diana and her. "This one is for math," she also said, placing a thicker paperback book atop of the science textbook. "This is your history book and this is your French book."

Two hardcover textbooks were placed on top of the former two books.

"You're to report here starting after the long weekend. Class will be held in the classroom across the hall. See Ms. Rivers next door to sign out these books and remember not to damage them... any more than they already are, please."

"Thank you," Diana replied without sincerity.

Diana took each book one by one into her arms.

"Alright, Dona, have a great summer," Meredith said with a sly smile as Diana turned to leave.

Diana didn't reply. Instead, she walked out of the office, into the loud hall, and around to the classroom behind the office. She got into a queue of several other students and waited impatiently for her turn to speak to Ms. Rivers. Diana looked behind her and out the door as the other kids stuck around with their friends or left to start their summer vacation while she was stuck behind.

"What are you in for?" a feminine voice asked.

Diana turned her gaze and looked at a wavy dark red-haired girl in front. She was shorter than Diana, but with a similar pale skin. She wore a yellow-black sweatshirt and jeans despite the early summer heat.

"Everything," Diana replied, showing her the four textbooks in hand.

"Jesus, did you fail every vital course in the year?"

"It's a long story... but in the least they let me slide through English since I did well on the final exam."

"That makes four out of five," the red-headed girl said with a smile. "I'm Moira by the way. What grade are you finishing?"

"Ninth," Diana replied. "I'm in ninth until I finish this catch-up."

"Oh, well, it'll be nice if you'll be in tenth with the rest of us next year."

"My name is Diana."

"Nice," she remarked. "Nice to meet you, Diana."

Moira turned around to face Mrs. Rivers. Diana kept her eyes on the two of them as she signed out her own book before turning around again.

"I'll catch you over the summer then, Diana," Moira said before darting off.

Diana looked over to her as she walked out.

"Next please," a clear feminine voice asked from behind her.

Diana turned around and over to Mrs. Rivers who gave a pleasant smile to her. She dropped her books on the desk.

"My, my," Mrs. Rivers said as she looked at the books.

Diana looked at the young woman. She had fair skin and curled brown hair. She lowered her glasses from atop of her head so that she could read the title of each text.

"It seems that you've had quite the unproductive year."

"I just moved here actually. I missed a lot and need to catch up before next year."

"No problem," she replied, writing down each book number. "Sign here."

Diana bent over and signed the paper. She then turned it back to Mrs. Rivers before taking the books back. Diana put them into her backpack that Charlemagne had the decency in buying her. The time they spent going out to buy basic school supplies was the nicest thing he had done so far for her.

"Thanks a lot... Diana," the woman said, reading the signature she left on the paper. "I'll see you back here after the long weekend. Have a good one!"

Diana took a step back and left the classroom. She entered the hall and went to her assigned locker she had for a short period and now needed to clear out. She opened it, took the notebooks that she had been using, and put them into her backpack as well before closing it and taking the lock with her. Diana looked around the strange faces that were her schoolmates. She then made her way out.

Once outside, she looked around for Charlemagne and the black sedan where it would usually be behind the many cars along the curb. He always parked far from the parents to avoid attention. Diana caught a glimpse of Tristan as she looked around from atop of the steps to the front entrance of the school. He was sitting with his friends along the sitting wall to a pen of vibrant flower and shrubbery at the side of the path to the sidewalk from the steps. They were laughing. Tristan caught Diana with her gaze as he continued to smile about whatever it was he was joking about with his friends. Diana knew the boys around him by now. It was Peter Huxley and Aaron Phillips (each son to respective adults that Diana also knew by now, the Phillips that led the school as principal and the Huxley that led Cabernet Industries).

Diana turned her gaze away as she caught Tristan's smile (even though it was not directed at her). She started to walk forward and saw Mrs. Phillip pass by, walking elegantly next to her and towards her son. Aaron straightened his back and stood up immediately as Peter addressed her presence.

"Mom?" Aaron questioned, causing the boys to try and contain their laughter.

"Are you boys behaving?" she asked with a sly smile.

Diana walked past and glanced over as he noticed Charlemagne waiting across the street. Tristan caught Diana looking at him one last time before she started to jog away. He then turned his attention back to his friends as Mrs. Phillips left.

"Nice job, faggot," Peter remarked as they continued to laugh at Aaron.

"Come on, let's get out of here," Tristan suggested, hitting Peter along the back as he stood up.

Diana continued to make her way towards Charlemagne without batting an eye behind her. Charlemagne leaned on his sedan impatiently as he watched Tristan and his eye contact towards Diana. His eyes only shifted upon Diana's arrival to him, which caused him to straighten up and unfold his crossed arms.

"Did you get all your books?" Charlemagne asked her, turning to open his door behind him.

"Yes," Diana replied, walking around to get to her side of the car. "Let's get out of here."

"My pleasure," Charlemagne said in his usual depressive tone, stepping into car.

Charlemagne ignited the engine and changed gears to drive. He lowered the parking brake and pulled out of the curb. Tristan watched from afar as the car drove off. He was on the sidewalk with his friends, saw the car turn the corner and then went back to paying attention to his friends. Diana looked out the window in thought as the two of them went back to the manor together to retire for the day.

Act 3, Scene 3

Diana rose from the couch where she had been doing some reading for history. She stretched as she heard the sound of the doorbell ringing. She put the book down onto the coffee table, inserted her bookmark where she left off, and got up. She looked around for a moment around the library for as much as she had momentarily transformed it. The white sheets were gone, but the place still lacked the healthy vice of a true library without the many books that used to be here. In the least, Diana dusted around to make the place seem less old and instead homelier.

The doorbell went off again. Diana hurried up, walked out, and went straight to the grand foyer to open the front door. She rolled her eyes and tilted her head forward as she recognized the figure behind the front door window. It wasn't who she expected to see on his fine mid-July morning.

"Hey, what's up?" Tristan greeted as Diana opened the door to his smiling face.

"Where's your guardian?" Diana questioned instead.

Tristan ignored her, pushed past, and walked in. Diana looked over to him with crossed arms against her white t-shirt. She looked over to Tristan in his dark beige shorts, tank top and exposed tanned arms, and frown on his face. He walked into the foyer for about two meters before turning around to face Diana. His eyes passed her and went behind. His hair was kept short. He also had black sunglasses atop with blue temples.

"Whoa, is that vase authentic?" he questioned, walking over and past Diana.

Diana turned around to look to Tristan as he approached a clay vase on a pedestal next to the left front door. He got too close as his foot hit the bottom of the pedestal, causing it to shake and vase to wobble and then tip over. The vase shattered upon impact.

"Oh crap!" Tristan remarked.

"Nice," Diana sarcastically replied without amusement.

Diana turned her gaze up and over to Charlemagne as he made his way downstairs with a lethargic appearance. Charlemagne wasn't in his traditional grey suit, but instead in a black one with a black briefcase in hand.

"Clean that up, will you?" Charlemagne requested as he passed Diana.

Charlemagne paused at the still open front door and turned around to face her.

"I'm going to the office for a bit and won't return for a while. Have whatever you'd like for supper, but please, no more takeout Chinese. I can't handle any more of that filth, I'm afraid."

Charlemagne put his hands around the doorknob, closed the door and went off. He left Diana alone with Tristan and the broken Roman vase.

"You lucky bastard," Diana said to Tristan as the two looked at each other in shock and awe of the moment. "He'd have killed me had I been the one next to that vase."

"Yeah, yeah, whatever," Tristan replied, taking a sigh of relief as he squatted and poked at the pieces. "No way we can glue this thing together..."

Tristan stood up and went back to the front door. He looked out and watched Cabernet leave out the front gate. Diana uncrossed her arms and walked over to stand next to him as the two looked out together. Each of them felt the evening sun against them as it poured in through the rear windows of the foyer. It was starting to darken outside with the sun starting to set on the other side of the county.

Charlemagne turned left from the driveway and towards the freeway. Headlights shined from the opposite direction once he was gone. Diana heard the sound of an engine switch on as well before Salmar's convertible drove forward and into the driveway.

Salmar pulled the parking brake up, shifted gears and shut the engine off before hopping out of his convertible and walking up the steps of the manor.

"Hey, sorry about sending Tristan," Salmar apologized to Diana. "I had to send him in first to make sure Charles was out, but I saw his car leave and Tristan not return, so I assumed you were left behind and it was clear. How long do you think we have?"

"He went to the office with a briefcase, so I don't know... an hour at best? That's usually how long he's ever out."

"Okay, I can work with that," Salmar replied. "I have a plan – a good one given that those Feds could show up any moment to take you away from this place."

"Yeah, I know," Diana replied, recalling that her two months were officially over tomorrow.

"As soon as those G-men take you, Charles will rush his way to the airport and board his private jet to Harlech. It's too soon..."

"Those pills you slipped did a real charm," Tristan remarked from where he stood at the broken vase. "The guy seems to be jumping with joy. Why don't you let him just do what he wants, huh?"

"Not now, Tristan," Salmar replied in an angry tone.

"It's true though..." Diana replied, "the part about the pills not working. I ran through the entire bottle and he hasn't even lifted a smile. I feel like he's gotten worse if anything. Tristan just dropped that expensive-looking vase and he didn't even raise an eyebrow about it."

"I see," Salmar replied, "then maybe I don't have a plan. I should have given him a heavier dosage..."

"What are we going to do?"

Salmar turned to Diana and said, "Come on, let's go to the study. It always helped me to think in there."

"Have fun," Tristan replied, taking his phone out and walking off.

Diana followed Salmar to the study.

"I don't have any fresh ideas," Salmar said as they walked through the library. "I was hoping that the pills would have corrected his depressive disorder, but it hasn't. They've given him a worse depression by the sound of it. I truly have no idea what could be the issue."

"What's wrong with him if the medication didn't work?"

"I don't' know... I'm not a psychologist," Salmar replied as they entered the study. "All I've convinced him to do was to not sell the mansion and let me inherit instead, but that's not enough. I don't have the money to buy enough shares to win a majority, nor the charisma to convince the other members of the board to rally behind me. Charlemagne is the dictator of this company and he's got a violent agenda."

"You're a lawyer, though," Diana argued. "Isn't there anything... 'lawyery' for you to do?"

"I'm afraid not. I have no proof that Charles is a danger to himself. I cannot just accuse him of being suicidal. The police need *hard* evidence to arrest him for psychological duress."

Both of them perked their heads over to the desk as the phone began to ring. Instead of rushing towards it, Salmar went quietly over and looked at the phone number. Diana watched as he murmured to himself and then picked up the phone. She watched as Salmar talked, agreed and nodded to what was being said on the other line before turning to face Diana at the other side of the room. He then hung up.

"That was..." Salmar paused for a moment and walked back over to Diana. "It was Alberta Child Services. Some clown called Gregson said he was coming to pick you up Sunday morning."

"Yeah... I'm really going to get sucked out of this place, I guess," Diana replied, sitting down in an armchair as she tried to relax from a sudden burst of anxiety.

"Don't you worry, kid," Salmar replied, walking over to her with alertness and kneeling down. "Forget about our scheming for a moment and let me tell you something. I heard from Tristan what you went through in the last years, and I got to say... it's tough losing the people you love. I know from personal experience..."

"Your wife?" Diana questioned.

"Yeah... my wife," Salmar admitted. "It was two years ago... I was alone for a long time after that. It sucked being alone, but I had my family to support me in the least (minus my brother). For you though... you lost everything so young and appear to be so strong to have gone through that and have had to handle Charles at the same time. What you did... helping me too, I admire that and feel bad for what he's done."

"Don't feel bad," Diana said, lowering her head.

"Don't you worry then. My brother is a selfish asshole. He's always been like that since he was little. I could go on and on about him, but right now, let's not make your efforts be in vain. We need to figure out a plan to make sure that the company isn't dissolved."

"What though? What can we do?" Diana questioned. "I have no idea... we've run out of time."

Diana looked at Salmar who was looking back at her. He was silent for a moment.

"What's your motivation for this, Diana? Why have you helped so far? I've offered you nothing, and yet you persist to help me unlike Tristan... what's in this for you?"

"What's in this for you?" Diana questioned.

"Isn't it obvious?" Salmar questioned with a sarcastic laugh. "Charlemagne is my older brother. What about you?"

"I... I don't know. I just want to do the right thing... Cabernet Industries is a good corporation, and there's not many like it around. It's the understanding I have that Charles lacks..."

"Very true," Salmar replied with a smirk. "You're a good kid, Diana. You know that, right? A little like my sister, Allodia. She and I also have this persistence you seem to have, it's good."

Salmar went quiet for a moment as he looked to the side.

"You've got another two nights here, I suppose, and then you'll be going to another home, right?"

"It appears so," Diana replied. "It won't be last, surely, as it won't be my first, or second, or third..."

"You've moved around a lot?" he questioned.

"Yeah... not a lot of owners seem able to tolerate me..." Diana replied. "I can understand though.... In fact, this mansion and town is the first place I've stayed this long in, really."

"Really...? I can't imagine. Any man would be lucky to have a daughter like you," Salmar said, smiling at her. "I know I would."

Diana nodded as she looked in front of her.

"In fact, I think I'd like to make that happen, Diana," Salmar said.

"What?"

"I'm serious. I want to make sure you never have to go through anything like that again, kid. No less after you've had to weather Charles of all people. He adopted you, and if he won't take responsibility of you, then I will. You're part of the Cabernet clan now, kid. We take care of our own... something that's been amiss with Charles."

"You... you don't have to do that," Diana replied. "What about Tristan?"

"Don't worry about him," Salmar assured her, standing up.

"Why? What's the motivation behind that?" Diana questioned.

"Well, it's only fair enough to be the same motivation you've had in trying to stop this sell-off of Cabernet Industries... because it's the 'right thing to do' and all that."

"Th-thanks..." Diana replied, turning her head to the side. "I appreciate that, but what do we do about Charlemagne? He's still going to sell the company, and worse... he's still going to kill himself afterwards."

"One step at a time. We need to focus on the company first," Salmar replied, turning around and stroking his chin. "We've misunderstood Charles and his condition. The medication should have worked... we screwed up – I screwed up. We don't have much time. We need to be tactical in this last move."

Diana watched as Salmar moved over to the model of King Island. He stood behind it and rested his hands on either side of the rim.

"I can't help my brother... we need to focus on Cabernet Industries right now. I need to seize Cabernet Industries,"

Salmar said, moving his finger over to pinch the top of the model of Cabernet Tower. "If we had the power the company had... the proof that he was not well, we could then get him the help he needs and can get at a psychiatric facility, but we don't... not yet."

The sound of a cellphone began to ring as Salmar finished his sentence. Salmar took out his phone to read it before popping his headset into his right ear.

"Give me some privacy. It's a client calling..." Salmar requested. "Go find Tristan and make sure he's not doing anything mischievous or something."

"Sure thing," Diana agreed, standing up and going for the door.

"Hello," Salmar said, "it's me."

Diana turned around as she got to the door. Salmar walked over to Charlemagne's computer and sat down. She took a deep breath, opened the door and then turned back forward to walk out. She went to the grand foyer as she heard a doorbell ring.

"What now?" Diana questioned as she went to the door.

Diana came to the grand foyer and met up with Tristan as she stood at the front door with a clipboard and pen. He gave the clipboard back and continued to look outside as Diana came over to join him.

"What the hell are you doing?" Diana asked him as they both looked outside.

Three delivery trucks with ramps extended were parked outside on the front driveway. Several workers were scrambling around, carrying boxes and tropical decorations of the sort.

"Salmar said that this place was his now since Charles was going wherever it was he's going, so I'm going to have a party in our new home seeing that we won't be moving in for a while. Can't I have a party? It's not going to be *your* home for a while longer, and I'm just sending the bills to Charles – he's loaded, right?"

"Now though?" Diana asked. "You're going to have a party *now?*"

"No, not now. This is just some stuff I ordered ahead of time. I was thinking next week or maybe Sunday once Charles leaves. Salmar has a business trip he'll be attending as well, so it'll be perfect."

The two of them stepped out of the way as workers began to pass through the front entrance with luau umbrellas, surfboards, tables with bamboo wickerwork, and all sorts of other tropical decorations. Two men also passed by with a large Tiki head.

"Are you going to stop me?" Tristan asked, turning to Diana.

Diana took a deep breath.

"Well, it's not like you can seeing that you won't be living here either."

"I can tell on you," Diana remarked, causing Tristan to frown.

"What's going on?" Salmar questioned, stepping towards the two from the library.

Diana and Tristan turned around to face him as additional workers moved in and the former out with more stuff.

"What's with all this crap?" Salmar questioned.

"It's for a party," Diana said ahead of Tristan, crossing her arms with a smug smile.

"A party?" Salmar questioned. "Wait... yes! A birthday party! My God, it's the 22nd of July tomorrow – that's Charles' birthday! If we can pull off a classic Cabernet-themed party, then we might just raise his spirit. Oh, Charles used to love parties. If we can immerse him in something that he used to enjoy, then maybe we can activate the old Charles again."

Salmar stepped ahead and out the door to go down the steps. The teens watched from within the mansion as Salmar blew a whistle with his fingers to get the attention of the workers around.

"Heyo!" Salmar yelled. "Could you get your crews to unload in the loading zone around the side of the house? Thank you!"

Salmar turned around and came back up the steps to pass the kids. He went towards the sitting room and further. The others followed him.

"You know, this might just work," Salmar said as they followed him towards the kitchen to go to the freight lift. "Can you two hide the stuff they left in the main entrance? Hide it outside or something. I'll get these guys sorted out in the cellars and move my car."

"Sure thing," Tristan replied, sighing.

Diana and Tristan left the kitchen closet as Salmar lowered himself. They made their way to the foyer and started to move some of the decorations through the narrow door behind the left staircase to the terrace. The two of them rolled the large Tiki head last and came back as another two trucks began to arrive as the last three left. Salmar was at the driveway.

"How many trucks did you call?" Salmar asked, looking over to Diana.

"Hey! Somebody order a dozen boxes of pineapples, coconuts and ice cream?" a deliverer asked from his truck.

Salmar rushed ahead over to him.

"Loading zone is over here!" Salmar said, pointing to the extension of the causeway going towards the garage.

Salmar walked back over and up the steps.

"The trick is to tell the drivers to park in the back when you call for deliveries," he told them. "Are there anymore incoming?"

"No," Tristan replied. "Here," he added, handing Salmar the invoices.

"Thanks," he replied.

"I think some catering trucks and light decorations will be here tomorrow," Tristan also added.

"I'll be around for that. I can take care of it," Diana replied, looking at Tristan.

Tristan looked back at her with a frown.

"I can also set everything up on my own if we're doing this party tomorrow," she said.

"No need. Tristan and I will be here bright and early to help you with that before this party kicks off? When were you thinking we should start?"

"I was thinking about noon until the evening," Tristan replied.

Salmar looked over to Diana for a response.

"Yeah, what he said. Let's call it one o'clock."

"Alright then," Salmar replied. "That'll give us a good morning to get ready."

"What if Charles finds out beforehand?" Diana questioned.

"Oh, I expect him to find out beforehand," Salmar replied, looking around the front lawn. "The thing is, he'll have nothing to do about it by then. Not even in this sunken spirit can the Charles I know refuse a party..."

"Okay, but how will we spread news about a party being held here?" Diana asked.

"Don't you worry," Salmar responded. "An event at Cabernet Manor spreads far and wide within seconds. It won't be long until we have hundreds to a thousand people trying to get in."

"Uh... perhaps we should keep it lowkey – more discreet," Tristan suggested. "I can send out invitations on social media to people within the town."

"Yeah, that can work too," Salmar remarked, clearing his throat as he looked forward and down the cliffside road. "I need you to do something more for me, Tristan. I'm going to need you to distract my brother a little while longer until I text you that all is clear. He needs to keep clear from the driveway. Keep him busy until then, okay?"

Diana looked outside as headlights approached the mansion from the left.

"Yeah, sure thing," Tristan replied feeling a little nervous over his role as the gates of the manor opened up.

"Alright then," Salmar said, tapping Diana on the shoulder. "Let's go to the garage and get this last shipment so the trucks can get out as quietly as possible."

"Yeah, okay then," Diana replied, looking over to Tristan as he left to handle the worst part alone. "Let's go."

Act 3, Scene 4

"Alright, Tristan. We can do this. Diana's been handling him for the last two months. I can handle him for fifteen minutes," Tristan said to himself.

Tristan continued to look over to Charlemagne as he drove into the manor and parked his car ahead. It was dark now. Lights had turned on around the mansion. Charlemagne exited his vehicle with his briefcase in hand, walked around the front of his car, and made his way up the steps of the manor. He looked over to Tristan and didn't change his dull expression as they made eye contact.

"Are you still here?" Charlemagne questioned, raising an eyebrow and walking past him as he stepped away.

"You weren't gone for very long," Tristan replied. "I haven't been here that long either."

"What are you doing here?" he asked.

"I'm... here visiting Diana," he lied as Charlemagne turned to face him.

Charlemagne loosened his tie as he looked at him.

"Close the door, will you? You'll let the bugs in," Charlemagne remarked, turning for a moment before stopping himself as he eyed the broken vase. "I thought I said to clean that up," he added, shaking his head before going to the library.

"You did," Tristan replied, catching up to him. "Diana said she'll clean it up – she went to go get a broom. Don't your worry about it, Mr. Cabernet."

Charlemagne looked over to Tristan with a raised eyebrow as he followed him in the library to his study.

"There's no need to call me 'Mr. Cabernet,' lad," Charlemagne insisted as he made it to his study with Tristan behind.

'I'm sorry, uh... Charlemagne..." Tristan corrected as Charlemagne opened the door.

"Still too formal, my boy," Charlemagne remarked from under the open doorway. "Try 'Charles' like everyone else. It's more appropriate."

"Alright then," Tristan replied, rushing over as the door closed behind Charlemagne. "Hey, wait up."

Tristan entered the study and looked over to Charlemagne as he went to his desk.

"What's up?"

"I'm busy at the moment. Why don't you go find the girl and talk to her?" Charlemagne replied as he opened his desk drawers and started to search around.

"What are you looking for?" Tristan questioned, slowly walking forward to stand near him.

"Papers," he simply replied as he searched his desk. "I have some important documents here to sell off the oil fields in north Alberta. I have to sign them off and scan them."

"Oh, that's nice..." Tristan replied, standing with his hands behind his back at the corner of Charlemagne's desk.

Tristan looked over to the computer screen on Charlemagne's computer. It displayed an open document that read atop 'Last Will and Testament of Charlemagne de la Cabernet.' Tristan took a deep breath before turning his gaze behind him. He looked at the replica of King Island and faced it.

"What's this?" he asked.

Charlemagne looked over to him, the model, and then sighed before saying, "It's a scale-model of King Island in Harlech."

"Oh, that's Harlech? The whole city?" he questioned, looking at the density with intimidation.

"No, it's much bigger than just that island. King Island is the densest for sure though. It's home to Cabernet Towers," Charlemagne replied, standing up from his desk and walking over to the table. "Right here, see?"

Charlemagne pointed to Cabernet Towers in the center. The logo of Cabernet Industries could be seen on the north and south sides of the tower. It was also the tallest tower in the entire city among all the other skyscrapers.

"It's nothing too special," Charlemagne remarked, going around the table to leave the room.

"Maybe not to you," Tristan replied, following him and into the library.

Tristan followed from behind as they continued in silence. Charlemagne made his way across the foyer with him following. He came close to the sitting room, causing Tristan to raise a hand to prepare to stop him. He lowered it instead as Charlemagne stopped, shook his head and turned around. Tristan caught up as they went up the stairs together to the second floor. They entered the foyer of the north wing when Charlemagne took out an old key from his pocket to unlock the door against the diagonal wall.

The door opened and Charlemagne went inside the dark room. The door creaked open and closed behind him to be left ajar. Tristan caught up and pushed it open. The door slowly pivoted and lights switched on as Tristan looked around the makeshift lab with awe. He looked at all the machinery, stations, equipment available and then over to Charlemagne as he sat down at a stool in front of an old computer monitor. He began to go through some paper atop of it.

"You have your own lab?" Tristan asked with surprise.

"Yes, but it isn't that impressive. It holds only the basics really. All of which will be donated to your school when I'm gone, I believe."

"Gone?" Tristan questioned, looking over to him as he searched papers and froze.

Charlemagne didn't reply and continued to search. Tristan looked away from him and back at the lab with amazement. He walked over to the chemistry table and looked at the distilling equipment and containers of various samples before going to the workbench with various tools lined up along a wide peg board. He picked up a stainless-steel cylinder, examined it carefully and tried to figure out what it was before putting it back gently.

"Ah, here it is!" Charlemagne remarked, causing Tristan to jerk his head back over to him. "Where's a pen around here?"

Tristan walked over to a table where there were some tanks, one of which had a dead spider and another with a live lizard, both with flora. He came over to the large machine in the corner next to Charlemagne with the large transparent chamber and metal reinforcements on the side. An extra cylinder was lodged on the far left, on the lower half of the cylinder. Various monitors were hooked up around the two rings at each third of the cylinder, and there was an apparatus extending from the center with a microscope eyepiece atop.

"What's this?" Tristan asked, placing both hands on the console slanted on an extension of the machine.

"It's a multi-use system I designed myself," Charlemagne said, turning his head over from the paper he was reading.

"What does it do?" Tristan queried, jumping his hands away from the console as it lit up.

"Well, lots of things," Charlemagne replied, standing up and walking over to Tristan. "It's useful in doing all sorts of tasks, experiments and the sort – a helpful aid in researching. It measures, collects information – let me show you."

Tristan moved away from the console so that Charlemagne could take over. He tapped the console and caused the disc inside to spin and be brought to the side of the chamber closer to Tristan before lowering into the antechamber.

"Sit at my computer and open the program at the top left of the screen on the desktop," Charlemagne instructed. "This device is remotely linked to my computer to upload data and to access the microscope settings in various configurations. Sit down at the stool and I can show you."

Tristan sat at the stool and clicked at the shortcut at the top left of the screen. The machine began to hum and the antechamber opened like a disc tray to a computer with the top half exposed and disc seen inside the machine in the center.

"Here, I've got a sample of a certain type of tissue from a certain type of animal. Have a look at it," Charlemagne said, taking a glass slide atop his console.

Charlemagne set it in the center, in a certain spot in the disc where a slide fit perfectly. He then turned around, tapped on the console, and caused the antechamber to close. The disc rose back up and came to the center of the tube. Charlemagne then walked over to the desktop where Tristan was looking at the screen. The program had opened up and showed a grey window.

"Click the microscope icon," Charlemagne instructed.

Tristan did so. It opened a black screen.

"Go to the top bar and select input. Choose 'main-source' and then pick magnification. Select '400x.'"

Tristan did so. The screen switched to showing a feed of the sample from the perspective of a microscopic camera inside. Tristan looked over to the chamber where an extension from apparatus in the center was centered right over the slide. He then looked back at the image.

"Do you see those strands bunched together?"

"Yeah," Tristan replied.

"Those are cilia exposed to methacholine. What you're seeing is mucous."

"Like... snot mucous?" Tristan questioned.

"Kind of. This is mucous derived from a protein known as 'mucin.' It reacts with water to puff up like a sponge. Here, it's not picking up bacteria and debris like mucous would in your nose, but instead, affecting a water gradient in the throat – this is a sample of tissue from the throat of a rat."

"Wow, that's amazing," Tristan replied. "What were you studying?"

"I wasn't studying anything. This type of tissue has already been studied by many and is well known in histology. I was simply bored and decided to try and mimic the gradient that drives water to the front of our throats to give us a clear air passageway when we lack water. Watch, I'll mimic it now."

Charlemagne went back to his console and tapped around. The machine hummed. Tristan watched as a robotic arm extended towards the slide with a very thin probe that extended towards the slide.

"Do you see the movement from the bottom to the top? I added a very thin drop of water to the bottom. The electrical gradient caused by calcium and sodium ions cause the water to go a certain direction – the same direction that draws water. Our body regulates which direction it needs water by influencing the ions in our body like potassium, sodium or chlorine."

"To achieve homeostasis, right?" Tristan asked.

"That's right." Charlemagne said, looking over to Tristan with a light smile. "I was trying to figure out with I could mimic such ionic gradients in dead tissue like this so I could try and mimic such ionic gradients with other ions, such as potassium and chloride together. I wanted to try and synthesize my own potassium chloride."

"Why?" Tristan asked, looking away from the monitor and towards Charlemagne.

"Uh, never mind that. I was unsuccessful anyways..." Charlemagne remarked, lowering his smile and turning his back to Tristan.

Tristan looked at him before looking back at the monitor.

"I didn't know our throats worked like that. It's amazing, really."

"Yes, it's one of the many ways our bodies fascinate us. Little ways that make the world go round and keep our complex bodies – an amalgamation of cells – together, unified and working together to be what we are."

Tristan paused from looking onto the computer screen and took out his phone as it briefly vibrated. He checked the message and noticed it to be Salmar in regard to the trucks being cleared. Tristan read it and then quickly put the phone back into his pocket as he turned to Charlemagne, who was fiddling with the console.

"Is medical research like this all that you do?" Tristan asked, looking around the various stations.

"No, not just medical. Not just scientific research either as a matter of fact," Charlemagne said, turning to Tristan with a pleasant smirk on his face. "I used to be an adventurer and explorer who searched every end of the earth and beyond to solve the unknown. My scope goes beyond the natural sciences to incorporate historical research, archeology and even sometimes paleontology. I'm also an inventor – I build my own gadgets, draft my own blueprints and schematics, and field test them myself. I used to do it all, but... but now I've slowed down and lost passion."

Charlemagne rested his jaw with his last sentence and dropped his smile to a frown as he looked down.

"I think that all sounds amazing," Tristan remarked with a smile on his face. "Salmar always talks about you as a mad man, but the way you make it sound – it sounds *really* cool!"

"Thank you," Charlemagne replied, cheering up again with a smile. "The last project I had worked on (and most likely won't finish) was on the human brain, you know. I was investigating whether the quantum processing in brain cells was the key to whether or not our minds held properties as a receiver and a transmitter – whether they're a transceiver. I only theorized as much as I could and didn't get much done. Perhaps you can one day take my place..." he said, looking over to Tristan as he placed one hand over the research machine. "You seem like an intelligent chap, and with Salmar as your guardian, finances will not be an issue in this country for pursuing your aspirations. You'll be going places for sure – better places than me."

Charlemagne looked at Tristan with pity. He simply nodded, tapped the top of his research machine, and then started to walk around to leave. He stopped at the end of the table, frowned and looked down. Tristan was watching him. Charlemagne looked back over to him.

"Don't stop pursuing what you dream, son," Charlemagne suggested, "but at the same time, remember that you'll eventually grow to feel empty inside even when those dreams haven't been complete. Some of us seek the greater things in life than settling down and having a family, but none of us that are normal do not wish to settle down with a special someone. I made that mistake, perhaps.... We can be remembered by some for the things we do, but the more meaningful memories and legacy lies in our own people. As men, we live and die, but as a family and beyond (our kin), we can be immortal. Your people are the most important aspect and should be most important aspect of everybody's life, my boy. Don't forget it."

"Yes, sir," Tristan replied, suspicious of Charlemagne's deep wisdom as he moved over to the door.

"What do you hope to be?" Charlemagne asked as he held a hand at the door and looked to him one more time. "Career-wise?"

"I want to be a doctor when I grow up," Tristan replied, looking over to him.

Charlemagne nodded before looking out the door as he said," That's good. A doctor is one of the most important careers out there. That's very good."

With those last words, he left. Tristan stood up from his stool and went after him. They entered the foyer when Tristan's cell vibrated in his shorts again. He took out his phone and read that Salmar and he were leaving. Tristan gave one last look over to Charlemagne in pity as he went around and disappeared to the other side of the second floor. He went downstairs instead to meet up with his guardian.

Diana stood under the door frame between the foyer and hall outside the library with her arms crossed. She saw Tristan approach the door and put his hand at the door handle. He first looked over at the vase and then over to Diana. He took a deep breath, opened the door, and left with a deep regret. Diana continued to frown as she uncrossed her arms. The door closed to leave her alone again. Tristan went off and into the night to meet up with Salmar. Diana stepped over to the vase and looked down at it. She then sighed and went to go get a broom to clean it up herself.

Act 4, Scene 1

"Oh, what on Earth is going on now?" Charlemagne questioned himself, listening to the loud boom of trucks backing in somewhere.

Charlemagne walked down the foyer staircase closest to his bedroom and over to the front entrance door to see Salmar at the foot of manor, directing a queue of trucks waiting outside the mansion. A truck at the bottom of the hill had its rear ramp open with workers taking out Hawaiian decorations to bring into the manor.

"Salmar!" Charlemagne shouted, causing him to turn around. "What the blazes are you doing?!"

"Charlemagne!" Salmar greeted, waving over to him. "Happy birthday!"

Salmar walked up the steps with open arms. Charlemagne held a deep frown as he looked to him. He stepped back and pushed his brother away.

"What's wrong?" Salmar questioned, dropping his smile. "I thought you loved parties!"

"I used to, Salmar... I *used* to," Charlemagne replied, "especially when I threw 'em, but I haven't felt the urge to in ages. This, however, is not for the *fun* of it. This is just to spite me!"

"Oh, come on now.... You know that's not true, brother," Salmar replied, putting an arm on Charlemagne's shoulder as he turned around and went back inside.

"Get these imbeciles off my property!" Charlemagne ordered, shoving Salmar's grip off of him. "I then want you out of here – I'm not dead yet – the house isn't yours yet."

Charlemagne was breathing heavily as he looked at his brother with a fierce expression. His eyes wandered to a courier behind Salmar, who caused him to turn around and go back upstairs.

"Are we still bringing in the banner?" the courier asked.

"Of course," Salmar replied with a confident tone, turning to him. "The party goes on! He'll see light soon..."

Charlemagne came to the corridor outside his bedroom and looked out the window. Various workers were placing decorations all around.

•

The late morning turned to late afternoon as Diana greeted the chef to grill the main course for the party. She then left the kitchen and came into the trophy room where he could hear the ambience of tropical music fill the house from the patio terrace.

Diana would have felt annoyed and anxious over the loads of young people swarmed outside, dancing to the music and swimming in the pool had this not been for a good cause. Tristan managed to do a good job in spreading the message about the party. Diana could see him with his friends, sitting down at a corner patio table with his friends on either side and a cold drink in his hands. He wore a pair of blue board shorts and nothing else. His tanned skin was exposed to Diana's sight as well as his slim, but mildly lean build for a fourteen-year-old boy. Around his neck was a gold necklace with a pendant of some sort. It was oval in shape. Diana only gave a quick glance to him as though she was annoyed with him.

The three of them were shirtless as much as the other men on the scene were, and the girls in swimsuits and string bikinis. Diana looked around for Charlemagne in hopes that he was at least having a good time (whatever that was supposed to look like). She couldn't find him. Diana wore a hula skirt over some shorts and a lime green sleeveless top. Her hair was also tied back.

The sound of a boy cannonballing into the pool caught Diana's ears as she flinched and some water hit her. She backed away to cast her gaze to the patio entrance from the foyer where Charlemagne had finally arrived in a black business suit with an unimpressed tone to his grim and sunken face. He looked ready to leave to Harlech at any second.

Charlemagne searched around briefly and moved his way to the catering. He looked at the food as she continued to look around. Diana made her approach.

"Where's my brother?" Charlemagne asked her.

"Uh..."

"I want to speak to him at once – I told him to pack this all up, and for whatever reason, there are a bunch of youngsters here that need to go home. He calls this a party – bah, this is the saddest sight I have ever seen."

"I don't know where your brother is, but I'll find him... just sit over here and wait."

Diana led Charlemagne to a seat and then looked around herself for a possible visual of Salmar. Instead, she gazed at Tristan again as a short silk-like blonde-haired woman made her way past the boys. Diana shook her head as Tristan began to flex for the girl. She lowered her sunglasses with one hand and held a pineapple-shaped glass in the other. She shook her head in disbelief with a wide pitiful smile before leaving. The other boys laughed at him.

Another girl came by, Vivian Huxley, the sister of Peter Huxley (who was one-year older than both Tristan and Diana). Tristan stood up as she approached. She had untied light-brown hair and was dressed in a bikini. Tristan and the boys smiled over to her as he put his arm around her waist as he got in close to her amusement. Diana retched at the sight of it and turned around. She caught a glimpse of Salmar in the garden. She then turned back over to Tristan as Vivian had disappeared and Tristan's friends were laughing at him about something. Tristan left them and went after Vivian who was at the other side of the terrace.

The party was beginning to become unfamiliar to even Diana as she looked around at all the cheerful and vibrant faces. She felt sad somehow. She looked over to Charlemagne as he continued to sit in his chair under the shade of a parasol above him, near the entrance to the trophy room, and with an expressionless face. She sighed and turned to go after Salmar.

Salmar closed his cellphone and put it back in his khaki shorts. He then put both arms on either side of the balustrades as he looked out to the garden and field beyond. Diana joined him as he took something from another pocket.

"It's not working," Salmar admitted with a frown as he looked to Diana.

"I figured," Diana admitted, resting her elbows on the balustrade. "Do you mind?"

"You smoke?" Salmar questioned as he brought a cigarette to his lips.

"All my life," she replied.

Salmar looked at Diana suspiciously as he lit his own cigarette with a steel lighter before handing the packet over to her. Diana took a cigarette out and passed it back to Salmar who gave her the lighter next. She brought the cigarette to her lips and lit it up.

"I didn't take you for a smoker," Diana said as she exhaled.

"Being a lawyer is a stressful job," Salmar admitted. "Being the brother to Charlemagne for forty-five years is even worse."

"Yeah, I feel you after being under his roof for just two months."

"Don't worry, kid," Salmar said, exhaling. "Tomorrow I'll make sure you're under my roof."

"Thanks again for that," Diana replied, putting the cigarette back to her lips.

The sound of beeping started to come out from Salmar's shorts. He lowered his hand into his pocket and scooped out his cellphone. He flicked the ashes from his cigarette as he squinted at the screen. Diana looked over to him as he exhaled towards the gardens and watched Salmar read what was on his phone before putting her own cigarette back to her lips.

"I've got to go," Salmar said in a frown, punching his cigarette out and putting his phone away in his pocket. "This party was a failure as I expected. I've got a call to make. I'll see you tomorrow, kid."

Salmar nodded to Diana before heading down into the garden, and around the right to head to the garage where his car was.

"Oh, wait!" Diana remarked to him, but he was already gone. "Your brother wanted to talk to you..." she finished saying in a quiet tone. "Damn..."

Diana exhaled as he gave a deep sigh. The smoke blew out from his lungs and over the flora in the garden beyond. With less than an inch left on her cigarette, she pushed the bud onto the top of the balustrade and went to go join the rest of the party. Diana passed the frowning gaze of Charlemagne and began to make her way inside, but not before bumping into Tristan who was in his board shorts and soaking wet.

"Hey, where've you been?" Tristan asked with a wide smile. "I was looking for you earlier. Come join me in the pool!"

"No thanks..." Diana replied, side-stepping to go around. "I'm not dressed to swim."

"Aw, don't be so shy, you silly goose," Tristan remarked, grabbing her by the wrist. "It'll be fun. Go get changed and come down before the sun starts to set."

"I'm good, thank you. I'll catch you later," Diana replied instead.

"What's got you so down?" Tristan questioned.

Diana shrugged and walked off. Tristan turned around and looked to her as she went inside through the trophy room entrance. His eyes then went over to Charlemagne. Tristan gave a sigh as he saw his idea of a role model sit with a frown on his face and arms crossed. Tristan ran his hands through his wet hair and looked back over to where Diana had disappeared to (inside the kitchen), but gave another sigh as he decided to go sit next to Charlemagne instead.

"Hey, how're you doing, Charles?" Tristan asked, squatting next to him.

"Could you believe Salmar?" Charlemagne bitterly asked with an angry tone. "I wish he'd just stop in his attempt to 'cheer' me up."

Tristan didn't know how to respond, so he didn't say anything in return. He looked to the side before looking back up to Charlemagne.

"Hey, Charles. Is it okay with I ask how you learned to do everything that you do? Science-wise?"

Charlemagne chucked and turned to Tristan.

"It's no big secret, my boy," Charlemagne replied with a smirk. "I just did. I did what I taught myself – the scientific method and onwards from there. I didn't learn it from high school or even university. I chose my own professors in the various authors I've read – from Oswald Spengler, Martin

Heidegger, to Johann von Goethe and Rudyard Kipling all the way back in time to St. Thomas Aquinas and St. Augustine of Hippo and even further back to Aristotle, Plato, and Socrates – these were the type of men that taught me – timeless men. This isn't to say that the presence and people in high school and college didn't influence me (some of them did and introduced me to some of these men), but the bulk of the effort came from myself. It was my will to learn and my will to go out there and immerse myself in the world that could be attributed the greatest. I *do* regret never finishing university, but this has more to do with the social aspect of being in a school environment – everything else can easily be done by anyone of their own accord. Of course, for what you wish to be trained in, dropping out isn't an option..."

"Yeah..." Tristan replied, smiling.

"But that isn't to say that all you'll have to read is your medical textbooks and the such. I encourage you to read more. Do lots of reading in all that is good and holy out there, and never stop reading, learning and expanding a healthy worldview of us as creatures of the natural world, please. You'll learn more on your own than what these professors can manifest upon you."

"I... I liked your idea about our minds as transceivers," Tristan said. "I had never heard of something like that before, and it really got me thinking all of last night."

"Good! That's good!" Charlemagne remarked with an encouraging smile. "Take these inspirations for all they're worth and look into these curiosities. It was from man's curiosity about the stars that got him to the moon all these centuries later! Embrace it!"

"I did!" Tristan replied with a smile. "I did my own research and just on the Internet I've learned so much more than I have at school. Quantum science offers so much that classical mechanics did not, and I think that us as conscious and advanced species may hold something more in our mind that could interact with perhaps another dimension too? Maybe I'm fantasizing, but-"

"No, that is all fine," Charlemagne said, stroking his chin as he thought. "There's no limit in our thought, and likewise, there should be no limit to our wonder. Our consciousness *is* truly a wondrous development as far as evolution has accomplished, and these questions are fair – modern science has become so obsessed with the empirical and provable that it has stopped asking the philosophical questions that can trigger research projects and such. I like where your mind thinks, Tristan. I do."

"Thank you," Tristan replied. "It means a lot that you say that, Charles."

Charlemagne looked at him with a tame smile. He nodded to him before waving his finger.

"Oh, that reminds me!" Charlemagne remarked. "If you have the time, go down to my private library and collect all of my personal research journals before they're thrown out. They should still be there provided that *brat,* Diana, hasn't thrown them out."

"You, uh... don't like Diana, do you?"

"No," Charlemagne replied, closing his eyes as he brought a hand to his forehead. "I... don't mind her, it's just... she's been a barrier to my plans. I can't help but blame her when I shouldn't. She's an orphan and has been through quite enough – I can see it in her eyes, really. She's lived a longer life than most children her same age. I admire her for it."

"So, why don't you feel bad about kicking her out?" Tristan asked.

"I do!" Charlemagne remarked. "I do, but... I have to."

"I can't say I agree with you on that," Tristan replied, causing Charlemagne to frown and look down. "You might be pleased to know that your brother is adopting her in your place."

"Really?" Charlemagne questioned, looking over to Tristan. "How... curious..."

Charlemagne looked off into the distance as he thought for a moment. Tristan looked at him. The two of them began to smell the odor of tobacco smoke. Charlemagne snapped out of his daze and shook his head.

"Speaking of the little devil," Charlemagne remarked. "I believe she's found where I hid her cigarettes and has them back."

"Back?" Tristan asked.

"Yes. I don't know how either. I locked them up in my lab when I took them off her in May. How did she get in? I've been strict in ensuring that the door remained lock."

"Are you sure it was her?" Tristan replied, standing up as he retained eye contact with Charlemagne. "Your brother smokes too, and we are at a luau with a bunch of teenagers..."

"Salmar smokes too?" Charlemagne questioned with a bit of surprise. "Hm, I didn't realize. Well, I suppose that makes the two of them a pair of dimwits. Regardless, I need to speak to him."

Charlemagne stood up and walked towards the source of the smell. He came to the top of the steps heading down into the gardens and looked around. Tristan followed from behind. Charlemagne didn't see anyone. Tristan turned his back on him for a moment as he looked around at everybody partying. He sighed and turned back around to Charlemagne.

"Listen, Charles," Tristan said, causing him to turn to him. "Why don't you head on in? Relax. It's your birthday. You don't want to be here – I'll make sure everything is taken care of with Salmar."

Charlemagne looked to Tristan and gave a faint smile as the two looked at each other.

"Thank you, Tristan," Charlemagne said. "I'll be in my study if you need anything."

"No prob," Tristan replied, letting Charlemagne walk past him and back inside.

Tristan looked around the party briefly and went over to the corner of the terrace to pick up his towel. He started to dry himself thoroughly before putting on his sandals and throwing his towel onto his patio seat. He picked up a hoodie and pulled it over to cover his skin before stepping inside the main foyer of the mansion.

It was quiet indoors. The echo of screams and laughter outside could be heard bouncing against the walls and through the empty space. Tristan made his way upstairs and walked into the small hallway before the makeshift lab to put his hands on the doorknob leading to his favorite room. He began to turn it after thinking it was still open from yesterday, and sure enough, it was. Charlemagne had truly forgotten to lock it.

Tristan walked inside and quickly went for the drawer underneath the computer to find a box of cigarettes with a health warning stretched across.

"Warning," Tristan whispered as he picked it up and searched for a lighter. "Smoking can make a boy become interested in you even though he shouldn't because he knows smoking is bad, but he wants to know more about you, and I should stop talking, because what the hell am I thinking – I don't like Diana..."

Tristan sighed as he couldn't find a lighter. He looked at the pack of smoke, squeezed it gently and then shoved it into his hoodie pouch. He then quickly closed the drawer and left the room to go downstairs.

"Or maybe I do."

Act 4, Scene 2

Diana went into the kitchen where a mess of trays had been left behind by the caterers. The room was dark as the sun started to set behind the mansion. She looked around the room and felt disappointed and sad. She went to a cabinet under the sink, took a black garbage bag out, and started to clean as she thought to herself. Diana filled the first bag and then sealed it shut as she moved over to the window looking outside. She saw a vintage black sedan with tinted windows parked about fifty meters from the garage door on the causeway. Diana moved away from the window and to the side to keep herself hidden.

Two men came out of the vehicle wearing blue pinstripe suits and matching fedoras under the same greasy black hair. Each of them were equally suspicious as they walked towards the garage door. Diana squinted to get a better look as they stepped their way forward and began to examine the garage door alongside the door next to it. Each of them had a briefcase in hand that they sat down. They could also be separated by their height and facial hair. The shortest of the two had a thin mustache versus the tallest with a thicker moustache.

Diana stepped away from the window as they started to prow their way into the stables through the garage door. She thought for a moment before crouching down and crawling towards the kitchen closet door. Once inside, she stood up and went to the door leading into the attic of the stables. Afterwards, she got onto a ladder and slid down to the ground floor of the garage. Diana then took cover behind Charlemagne's black sedan as she tried to listen to the mobsters. She came to the corner and could hear the rustling of metal tools as they fumbled with both doors still. Diana brought her hand down to touch the flagstone floor to get a better look around the corner before she suddenly jolted over the touch of a hand on her shoulder.

"Jesus Christ!" Diana shouted in a hush, turning around to see Tristan as he came up to her and knelt down behind.

"Howdy," Tristan said.

Diana hushed him and put her hands over his mouth. Tristan looked at her with curiosity and wide worried eyes. He took her hands by the wrist and gently lowered them.

"What are you..."

A sharp snap broke his sentence as Diana jerked her head over to the door and stood up. She took Tristan by his hand and rushed him over to hide behind a stall. They got around the corner as the front door flew open and hit the adjacent wall.

"Couldn't you have been a little more quieter?" one of the crooks said in a low voice.

The other hushed his partner.

"I got impatient," the other replied in a deeper voice.

"Who are these guys?" Tristan whispered to Diana.

Diana shrugged as she squatted at the corner of the stall and peaked around to get a sense of what they were doing. She could feel her heart beating hard and could hear Tristan breathing behind her as he was squatted right behind her. Diana backed off and pivoted to face Tristan instead.

"What the hell are *you* doing here?" Diana asked in a whisper, looking over to Tristan's smirk as he rummaged in his pouch.

"I wanted to give you this," Tristan said, presenting her pack of cigarettes in his hand.

"What?" Diana questioned. "How did you..."

"What're you doing?" one of the gangsters said in his faux Italian-American accent. "You've got to rewire the black one to make this work."

"Hey, who's the expert here? You or me?" the other replied in his deeper accent.

"Neither of us, you sack-of-fettuccini," the first said. "Now hurry up before we get caught. You'll ruin everything."

Diana looked over to Tristan and back around to the corner to focus on the gangsters. She watched the two crooks as they went over the front of the sedan with the hood up. They were fumbling around with the engine. Diana quickly jerked herself back and into Tristan as she barely managed to evade being spotted by one of the gangsters that had turned his head back.

"I think I saw something," one of them said.

"You probably just saw a rat," the deeper-voiced one remarked.

"Yeah, it was probably nothing."

"Move over," Tristan complained over Diana being too close to him.

"You move over, genius. I barely have any room here. You've got an entire meter behind you," Diana replied, pushing him back.

Tristan fell back into the metal bucket that was blocking him from going further. The rattle caused Diana to cringe.

"Rats?" the deeper-voiced one questioned.

"Go take a look," the other requested.

"Nice, you idiot," Tristan said.

"Be quiet," Diana replied to him, hugging the stall fence as she thought for a moment. "Okay, stay here," she said, looking over to Diana. "Protect my smokes, will you? And get help."

"What are you – Diana!" Tristan whispered, watching her stand up and walk out into the middle of the aisle.

"Hey, it's just a kid," the short deeper-voiced mobster said, causing the other to turn around from the car.

Diana looked over to them. One of the briefcases was on the ground next to the taller gangster, while the other was open and on the ledge of the car with tools inside.

"Nice tools you have there," Diana said. "What are you fellas' doing to Mr. Cabernet's car?"

"Shut your pie hole," the taller one said. "We can't leave no witnesses. Grab 'er!"

"Yeah?" Diana questioned, distancing her feet. "Come and get me!"

Diana ran forward and towards the shorter gangster, grabbing him and tackling him onto the ground.

"Whoa!" the taller one cried out, standing back.

Tristan watched from around the corner as Diana punched him mercilessly. The taller one knelt down, opened the second briefcase, and took out a Thompson submachine gun out. Tristan's eyes widened as he saw the automatic weapon come out and be pointed up into the ceiling, ready to fire with the tall one's finger on the trigger.

"Let 'im go or I'll make you into Swiss cheese," the gangster threatened.

Diana looked over to him with the gun and panicked. She got off him and stepped back. He pointed the gun towards her as the shorter one recovered.

"Don't just lie there – tie her down!" the tall one said.

The deep-voiced one rolled over and stood up. He took out some twist ties from one of the briefcases and went over to Diana.

"Vicious little thing, ain't she?" the tall one said, lowering the gun once her arms were tied behind her. "Take the gun so I can plant the other."

"No way," the other replied. "One is good enough. We got to get out of here in case someone else heard us!"

Tristan moved back and tried to find his cellphone on him. He didn't have it. The gangsters picked up their tools and closed the hood of the sedan.

"Let me go, you son of a bitch!" Diana cried out as she squirmed her wrists around.

"I'll see this one over the river once we're through," the shorter one said, picking up his suitcase and pushing Diana forward. "Come on, move with us and you don't get hurt."

"I'll kill you!"

"Yeah, but where's your Tommy, huh?" the taller one replied.

"Diana," Tristan whispered to himself as he watched from around the corner.

Tristan stood up and went around the corner of the stall fence once they left out the door. He ran over and hid at the side of the door as they pushed Diana into the back of their car before getting in the front. The taller one sat in the passenger seat while the smaller one drove.

"Hey!" Tristan shouted, coming around the corner.

"Oh shoot! You see?" the taller one remarked, looking behind him as he saw Tristan. "Hit the gas!"

"Hey!" Tristan shouted again as the car drove forward.

Tristan started to sprint towards the car. He eyed the license plate and scooped a rock to throw it at the car. It hit the rear window and left a crack.

"Diana!" Tristan shouted as he got to the end of the property.

"Son of a bitch!" the deep-voiced one said as he drove. "That son of a bitch!"

"Keep your cool," the taller one replied. "Just drive and get us out of here!"

Tristan felt the blood within in him flow as adrenaline hit. He felt surged to continue running, but the car was already more than a hundred meters down the road. He looked around and then back over to the gate as it started to shut. He quickly ran back inside and went towards the garage. He came to Charlemagne's car and lifted the hood to find what the mobsters had done. They had planted a small device along the side of the engine attached to a packet of white moldable material. The device was attached via wires to the battery of the car, which also had wires inserted into a metal object lodged into the moldable clay-like material. Tristan impulsively detached the metal object and left the bomb useless. He then turned around and found a bicycle at the side of a stall fence near the garage entrance. Tristan went over, picked up the bike and brought it over to the exit. He hopped onto the seat and began to peddle his way onto the road and away after Diana.

Charlemagne watched from his computer-screen as he stumbled upon Tristan exiting through the garage. He watched him leave and then went back to the feed of the stables. He rewound the footage and replayed the entire scene at high speed to get the gist of what had just occurred. Without hesitation, he grabbed his phone and called the police before bursting back outside to call off the party and order everybody home. Charlemagne then came to the front entrance as the police arrived with a bomb-detail that went to the garage. He looked around the front of the yard with a worried face before looking to the police chief approaching him.

Act 4, Scene 3

"You two scared or something?" Diana cried out from the backseat as the mobsters drove away from the manor and went across the river.

"Keep it down back there!" the deeper-voiced mobster yelled back as he drove into town.

"I could take you two chumps any day. I grew up fighting on the streets. I can beat the rustic crap out of you in less than two minutes!" Diana threatened.

"Forget about 'er, Louie," the taller brother replied, lighting a cigarette before cranking the window open.

The mobsters continued to drive along. They went straight through downtown Allabrese when the sun finally set. The car turned north before turning again not too far from the outskirts of the town. They had arrived at a medium-sized construction site and stopped outside of a portable office.

Each mobster got out of the car with their briefcases. The taller thug opened the door for Diana to get out. After waiting a short minute, he got impatient and reached in to drag her out. Diana tried to kick him, but instead the mobster grabbed her by the ankle and pulled her onto the mud.

"Get up and start walking," the taller one threatened as he pointed the Tommy gun at her.

"Screw you!" she replied.

The taller mobster started to shoot into the sky to spook Diana. She kept her head down until it was over before looking over to him. She got onto one knee and carefully stood up. The thug pushed her forward and towards the portable where Louie waited atop the steps and at the door.

The two of them joined him as he opened the door. They pushed Diana in first before closing the door behind them. The office had a mustier smell than the library at Cabernet Manor. Diana looked around the place, scanning each detail with her eyes before she was pushed onto the ground by Louie. Diana looked up as they took their hats off. She went back to looking around.

The office had a turquoise carpet and plain grey walls with desks around, books stacked and blueprints stretched out. The area was small and rectangular. The taller gangster fetched a foldable chair to cast in the middle of the room before he picked up Diana and threw her towards the seat.

"Call the boss," Louie said, pointing the gun over to Diana as the other finished restraining Diana to the chair with a rope.

"Will do," the other replied, standing up from Diana to walk over to a phone on the desk.

"You guys are pathetic," Diana mocked. "Weak and scared to the bone."

"Shut it before I have to tape that mouth of yours!" Louie barked, picking up the Thompson rifle on the desk as the other had the phone in hand.

"Where'd you guys find that relic?" Diana remarked, laughing. "A vintage Italian mafia shop? All the contemporary mobsters are using AK-47 nowadays."

The mobsters ignored him as she gave another chuckle.

"Boy, this town really is stuck in the past or something," Diana remarked.

"Shut up!" Louie yelled, walking over to her and hitting her in the cheek with the butt of the Thompson gun.

"Hey, boss. It's Danny," the taller one said. "We planted the package, but, uh... have hit a little snag with a hostage. We got caught and kidnapped some little girl that saw us do everything. What should we do with her? Wait it out with her?"

Louie glared at Diana with anger before turning over to his partner. Diana fell silent momentarily over the sharp pain.

"Understood," Danny replied. "We'll sit tight until then."

Danny hung up and took out a pistol from his blazer.

"Boss says to wait a moment," Danny explained to his partner. "He's going to call us back once he figures out what to do with the kid."

Diana laughed before saying, "You two don't even know what you're doing, do you? What a joke!"

"God! Why don't you just shut it, huh?" Danny said to Diana as he walked over to her with his pistol.

Diana quieted down as she eyed the pistol in hand. She tried to squirm in her ties but could barely move her arms around with the rope that bound her to the chair.

"All units, this is on-site security at the warehouse construction site," a voice said on the radio. "I think we've got intruders on the premise."

"Ah, shoot," Louie remarked. "Alfredo probably doesn't know we're here. Talk to operations and let them know of our status on the site."

Danny went over to grab the radio.

"Negative, security and operations. Task Team is on-site," Danny said.

"Affirmative, Task Team," a different voice replied. "Operations reads you."

Danny waited for a moment before looking over to Louie.

"Alfredo, this is Danny. We're here with you, don't worry about it. Do you copy?"

No response came.

"Alfredo, are you there?" Danny asked again.

"I don't like it," Louie said, stepping away from Diana and over to a cabinet behind him. "Grab a gun and go out there to find out what's going on."

"Me?" Danny questioned, looking over to his partner.

"Yeah, you," Louie replied. "Hurry up."

Danny walked over to the cabinet as he put away his pistol. He took out a Thompson rifle and two magazines. He loaded the gun and then went over to grab a portable radio and his hat.

Diana looked at the nervous face of Louie as he was left alone. They were both anxious, but for differing reasons. Diana had resolved herself into silence as she felt her heart pound against her chest.

"Louie... I just found Alfredo. He's out cold!" Danny remarked over the radio.

Louie lowered his gun and walked over to the H.A.M. radio on the desk. He picked it up.

"Are you kidding me?" Louie remarked, turning over to Diana. "How? Who? Find them!"

Diana raised her eyes over and looked to Louie as he started to tremble with his finger over the trigger.

"Danny?" Louie questioned. "Danny? Are you there?"

The radio was silent. Louie lowered it and went over to grab a portable radio. Diana could see the sweat drop from his combed-back black hair. Louie raised his arm over his forehead to wipe the perspiration before he put the radio into his pocket and glared to Diana. He left the room and went outside.

The silence in the office was eerie, but better than the company of either mobster. Diana could hear her own rapid breathing and still feel her heart pumping hard. Her eyes darted around the room before jerking back to the door as it opened. She gave a sigh of relief as she saw the familiar strawberry-blonde boy approach her.

"Tristan!" Diana remarked, squirming in her ties. "Get me out of here!"

"Hold on," Tristan replied, running towards and behind her. "I'll get you out of here."

"What did you to the others?" Diana asked as Tristan struggled with the rope.

"Nothing much," Tristan replied. "I just snuck around and knocked them out with a choke-hold from behind. My dad was a cop and taught me that kind of stuff."

"Funny," Diana replied. "My father was a criminal..."

The two of them jerked their heads over to the door as they heard the wooden steps creak. Tristan found some scissors and cut the plastic ties keeping her wrists together. He tried to cut the rope with the blade of the scissors next.

"Don't. There's no time," Diana said to Tristan.

"I can almost get it," Tristan insisted with determination as he continued to cut through.

"No," Diana replied, squirming harder. "Please -- just hide so that you can at least escape. One of us is enough."

Tristan paused for a second and heard the doorknob turn. He looked around, entered a cabinet behind him and shut it. Diana jerked her head over as Louie arrived. He ignored her and walked past to get to the desk with the phone atop. Diana squirmed in her ties, hoping the minor incision that Tristan had started might snap. Instead, she froze as she heard sirens approaching from the distance.

"No, not the pigs..." Louie said to himself, picking up the radio instead.

The phone rang. He lowered the radio and picked it up with his sweaty hands.

"H-hello?" Louie asked. "Giovanni - this is Luigi. Daniel is out cold. I'm on my own – yeah."

Louie raised a finger to look out the blinds as red and blue lights got closer and closer.

"Okay, I understand, sir. Sorry. No. We'll be over there pronto, don't your worry. Thank you."

Louie hung up and went over to Diana as he took out a knife to cut her free.

"We're leaving!" Louie remarked, grabbing her by the wrist as they made their way out.

Tristan peaked out of the cabinet as they walked out the door. He left as soon as they left and walked over to the door to hide around the side. The black sedan drove off with Diana in the back and the police cruisers arrived too late.

Act 4, Scene 4

"This is turning into one hell of a birthday," Charlemagne said to himself as he pulled into the construction site of a new Obelisk Paper Mill.

Charlemagne looked around the scene and could see two cuffed gentlemen in navy blue pinstripe suits being thrown into separate police cruisers. He looked around some more and found Tristan with an emergency blanket around his back, legs pivoted outwards as he sat in the rear of a car with two police officers and chief facing him.

"What's happened?" Charlemagne asked in his panic.

"They... they took Diana," Tristan explained in a disheartened tone.

Tristan told the crowd about the mobsters breaking into the garage to plant a bomb in Charlemagne's car. He then told them about how he peddled after the mobsters from afar and got her. He told them he knocked out the thugs and tried to free Diana but failed to.

"Well, that's quite a story, kid," Chief Phillips replied, raising his cap to scratch his head.

"It's the truth!" Tristan shouted at the brown-haired mustached chief.

"Easy, Tristan," Charlemagne replied, squatting down and putting a hand on his shoulder. "I believe you. They should believe you too since they've seen the security footage at the manor. Why don't I take you home? Salmar must be worried about you."

Charlemagne stood up and looked at the chief and two officers at his side with a serious glance.

"Find the abductor of my adopted-daughter, please?" Charlemagne asked.

"We'll do what we can, Mr. Cabernet," Chief Phillips replied, backing away with the other officers.

Charlemagne looked back over to Tristan who held his arms together for comfort. He shivered in the cool summer night.

"Mr. Cabernet doesn't sound too stoked on us finding his 'adopted-daughter,'" an officer remarked to his partner. "Maybe we should be questioning him?"

Charlemagne tightened a fist, but didn't say anything. He pretended like he didn't hear it as his frown stretched. Instead, he squatted down and put a hand on Tristan's shoulder.

"Come on, get up," Charlemagne said in a warm tone. "I'll take you home to rest."

"What about Diana?" Tristan questioned in a sad tone. "We need to help her!"

"The police are busy and will do whatever they can at the moment. Don't worry."

Charlemagne stood up. Tristan followed. The two of them walked over to his sedan where Charlemagne opened the passenger seat door to let Tristan in while he got his cell phone out to call his brother. Charlemagne raised his mobile phone to his ear while the cops looked around the construction site for further evidence. The ringing of the phone filled Charlemagne's ears.

"What have I done?" Charlemagne said under his breath. "This is all because of it – I should have just left it all to Salmar like it says in my will. Now this... the Medici gang after the people around me and my own life..."

"I'm sorry," a female monotone voice answered, "the number you are trying to-"

"Oh damn!"

Charlemagne hung up from the voice mail and looked around the crime scene one last time before getting into the car to look over to the burdened face upon Tristan. He started the engine, brought the parking brake down and shifted gears to reverse out and drive forward to Salmar's home.

"I don't want to go home," Tristan said as they went down the country road. "I want to go help and find Diana."

"I know you do, Tristan," Charlemagne replied, tensing his hands on the steering wheel, "but there's nothing you can do to help the police. We don't know where they could have taken him."

Charlemagne continued to drive back into town before making his way to the freeway. He drove along the country road heading east of Allabrese to get to his brother's home.

There wasn't a single light on at the ranch home of Salmar Cabernet. Charlemagne left the engine on as he shifted gears and brought the parking brake up. He got out of the car and walked over to the front door. He knocked on the door several times before stepping back in defeat.

Tristan watched from inside the car as Charlemagne walked back into the vehicle. He stopped in front of the car as he took out his phone. Charlemagne swiped his phone to unlock it and began to play a voicemail left mere minutes ago.

"Hello? Charlie, if you get this message then please, please help us. I was kidnapped by some mafia men and they've got me hostage at the abandoned coal mine near Linz Mountain. You should know where that is – it's you after all. I only managed to get free, but – oh God! They've found me – please help!"

Charlemagne pushed his phone away from his ears as static blurted out before everything went silent again. He put his phone away and went back to the car. He got inside and tapped on a console next to the steering wheel to phone someone.

"What is it?" Tristan asked in hope.

"I just got a message..." Charlemagne replied as the speakers of the car rang. "You're staying with me for the night, understood?"

"What happened?!" Tristan demanded to know.

"Hello?" a voice picked up and could be heard on the car stereo.

"Chief Phillips, this is Charlemagne de la Cabernet. I just received a voice message from my brother, Salmar. He's been kidnapped by more of these Medici gangsters and taken to the abandoned coal mine near Linz Mountain. I'll see you there."

"Understood, Mr. Cabernet. I'll be there with some of my boys as soon as possible."

Charlemagne hung up and put on his seatbelt.

"Kidnapped?" Tristan questioned as Charlemagne shifted gears and lowered the parking brake. "We... we got to do something!"

"I already told you-"

"Why?!" Tristan shouted at Charlemagne as they backed up. "Why are you such a stone-cold old man?! Why do you honestly not care about anybody but yourself? You maverick anti-social psychopath!"

With the sharp words from Tristan's mouth, Charlemagne hit the brake as they were speeding along the dirt road. The car made a sudden stop as Charlemagne turned to Tristan.

"I told you! There's nothing for us to do! This is a police matter – and it's being handled by the police! Don't you think that I want my brother to be free? Don't you think that I love my brother? Don't you also think that I want Diana to be free too? We're in the middle of a large situation, Tristan – a situation of which probably involves my company and the prejudice of a family you've probably never heard about, and their vengeance against not being able to take part in the auction of my company. I have a million more problems in my life next to this, and if you think this tug will move me as much as it is moving you, then it is because you are both so young and naïve that you've only started to live and learn about the dismal situation of the world."

Tristan didn't immediately say anything in response. He instead shook his head and looked forward as the car accelerated.

"I thought you were different from your brother. I thought I understood you," Tristan said. "I at least *thought* I was beginning to understand you. I guess I was wrong. They were right about you all along."

The car began to slow down to a calm pace as they arrived at the freeway. Charlemagne took quiet, but deep breaths that Tristan could here anyways. He continued to drive down and make his way towards the abandoned mine. They passed through downtown Allabrese, turned north and started to make their way towards Linz Mountain – a low elevation mountain north of the town and east of the river. It was surrounded by a light forest, which acted as the outskirts of the north border of the county much as the forest past the Cabernet Mansion acted as the west border.

Charlemagne drove along a road that went uphill but continued forward at a sign that said to go right for Linz Mountain. The sight of police sirens filled the scene ahead with their vibrant flashing lights. The tall grey facility had a steel-chain fence around it. The gates were open with tracks from the many police cruisers fresh in the dirt. Two police cars were parked at the gate and allowed Charlemagne inside. He followed their direction deeper into the site. He drove to the rear of the main building where the other cruisers were parked around the rim of a large black pit. Charlemagne parked the car and got out to look around.

The entrance of the mine at the bottom of the pit was lit up by large search lights brought by the police. Dozens of large rocks blocked the entrance. Tristan got out to get a better look as Charlemagne looked to him.

"We got here as soon as we could," Chief Phillips said to Charlemagne as he walked over to him. "We heard a large blast on our way over – we figured it was the blast that sealed that tunnel given that it's supposed to be open. Medici Construction has a contract with the city for the construction of the waterworks expansion. I have a team working on an alternate way in, but it'll take time – lots of time seeing that we don't have the explosives to breach."

"Have those men in custody spoken about what's going on? I knew they're members of the Medici gang and that they're responsible."

"Not that I am aware of, but yes, it appears this may have ties to the gang," the chief replied. "What does that family want with you? Do you have an unsettled score with them?"

"You know that my family deals clean, chief," Charlemagne said, turning to him with a strict face. "Have we heard any demands yet?"

"Not yet. They've been silent."

"But they *can* contact us. Salmar was able to contact me," Charlemagne said before thinking. "I can understand *why* they kidnapped Salmar as a means to get to me, but why haven't we heard from them?"

Tristan looked over and rested his hands gently on the police tape hanging around the edge of the pit, tied to orange reflective safety poles scattered about. He took a deep breath and felt the fear in his throat as he thought about the endless determination he had to save Diana.

"I better take the boy home," Charlemagne said, turning away from the police chief.

"Will you return?" Chief Phillips asked.

Tristan looked over to the two adults. Charlemagne gave him a serious and judgmental glare before looking back to the police chief.

"If they speak up, then call me, but until then, there's no point for me being here and it's just upsetting the boy," Charlemagne replied, looking back over to Tristan before going to his car. "Come on."

"I want to stay!" Tristan yelled to him.

"Enough!" Charlemagne shouted in response, starting to get heavily annoyed. "We are leaving!"

Tristan shook his head and walked over to the car to get inside. Charlemagne backed up and drove out of the construction site to head onto the freeway. Tristan crossed his arms and held a deep frown over his face. He also held a deep desperation to do anything to save Diana... the street orphan that had made a deep impression on Tristan ever since their first encounter at school.

Act 5, Scene 1

The black sedan pulled into the Cabernet Manor driveway, didn't stop atop the hill and base of the front entrance, but instead drove to the side to continue going forward along an alternative route to the right. The car approached the garage doors whereby approximately alone (like the front gate) the doors opened for the car to drive through. He made a smooth slow down inside the garage and a perfect stop before shutting the engine and looking over to Tristan with his arms crossed, face slightly wet along the cheeks from where he had been crying. He looked more serious now than Diana over the last two months.

"So, that's it then?" Tristan complained.

"What is?" Charlemagne questioned.

"We're not going to do anything? We're not even going to stick around to show our support? Nothing?"

"It's a police matter," Charlemagne retaliated, moving out of the car as the garage shutters closed. "They'll tell us if they need me, but they don't right now. It's at a stalemate and there's nothing that even they can do right now."

"They offered us to stay regardless!" Tristan immediately replied, getting out.

"Which would've been redundant," Charlemagne said before Tristan could finish speaking. "Look," he added, turning to face Tristan. "I offered you a bed for the night until they get Salmar out, so please, don't make me regret it."

"Oh, do you expect me to bow down for generosity?" Tristan replied as Charlemagne went to the elevator to go upstairs. "You're Charlemagne de la Cabernet! Don't you have anything?! There must be *something* around here that you could cook up to go after those criminals."

"I'm not the police!" Charlemagne yelled at him as Tristan went deeper into the garage. "Where are you going?" he questioned, stepping off the freight elevator.

Charlemagne entered the stable once more and looked over to Tristan as he examined each stall for what was there.

"What're you doing?" Charlemagne questioned with a bit of disbelief as Tristan went from stall to stall.

"You must have something," Tristan replied with desperation in his voice.

"Like I said," Charlemagne said again, "this is a police matter and far from our responsibility or jurisdiction."

"What's this?" Tristan asked as he tossed up a white sheet that was over a large mechanical beast at the end of the room.

"Oh please," Charlemagne scoffed, turning his side slightly away from what he had found.

Tristan pulled the white sheets away from the metal beast that a Second World War-era Panzer King Tiger Tank. The tank was large but neutered. The main cannon was missing and was instead rigged with the drill and vices of an excavator.

"Why do you have a *tank*?!" Tristan questioned.

"It's not a tank," Charlemagne retorted, taking a step forward. "Not anymore. It's an excavator. I could never get it to start up and work with the drill, and I wanted to use it to drill into some exposed rock nearby."

Tristan walked forward to run his hands over the diamond-tipped drill in front of him before he went around to climb over and onto the machine.

"Where do I open it?" Tristan questioned before realizing the turret head wasn't removed as much as the barrel of the cannon was. "Where's the cannon?"

"I had to remove it for legal purposes," Charlemagne remarked, observing Tristan.

"Ah, here's the engine," Tristan said, squatting down and opening the hatch atop the tank.

Charlemagne looked over to the tank and shook his head over the thought of getting the vehicle to start.

"If there's anything I knew about fixing cars with my dad," Tristan said, beginning to motivate himself whilst clenching his teeth as he searched the engine, "it's that the main problem is always... the oil."

"I already tried the oil," Charlemagne replied.

"Pass me some tools over," Tristan requested as he fumbled inside.

Charlemagne walked into the next stall and picked up a red toolbox sitting on a table. He then came back around to hand them to Tristan as he fooled around with the tank engine.

"I've fixed cars before, but this is no car I've ever seen," Tristan commented, rising up to look into the toolbox. "Thank you."

"That's because it's not a car – it's a tank with an engine as old as my own folks."

Tristan gave Charlemagne a plain look as he took out a wrench and then delved his face back in.

"Oh, like that'll do much," Charlemagne criticized as Tristan tried something.

Tristan ignored him and instead focused on tightening a couple of loose bolts whilst looking around for other possible problems.

"Are they both connected at the moment?" Tristan asked before bringing his head up.

"As far as I know," Charlemagne replied, moving to get off the tank. "It's got the fuel. It's got the oil. I could never solve the true issue, however."

"Hm," Tristan thought. "If only the drill isn't working then maybe the engine is having trouble powering the two simultaneously."

"I could see the logic in that, and I've also considered it," Charlemagne remarked. "I removed the radio set that was said to cause issues with the engine and battery, and I also changed the battery because it was exhausted when I bought it. The bloody thing could barely even start at the beginning – I began to think that perhaps I was overextending my wishes for this piece of machinery."

"Well, if the battery is new then this drill could be posing the same issues the radio sets were posing. Something is upsetting her if she doesn't want to start up."

Tristan reached around.

"What are you doing?" Charlemagne asked, crossing his arms.

"I need to examine this tube. Not enough fuel could be getting into the girl because of a clog."

"A clog..." Charlemagne mocked. "Listen, boy. This isn't some dame on an operating table or even your standard automobile. This is an armored war machine that is beyond your understanding. And besides, you're taking it out the wrong way and will make this thing more unsellable than it already is. Move over."

"Then quit your yacking and help me out," Tristan replied.

Charlemagne climbed up and knelt down next to Tristan.

"Oy, give me that spanner," Charlemagne said, taking the wrench from Tristan's hand.

Charlemagne lifted the cylinder block and then gently began to remove the attached pipe. He handed it to Tristan before digging deeper.

"Don't bother examining that pipe," Charlemagne replied. "I've found something else that might be the issue."

"What's up then?" Tristan asked, putting the pipe aside to get a look himself.

"I think the radiator hose is broken. The drill not working could be because the tank overheats too quickly."

"A broken hose would be too extreme. Maybe it just has a kink or something."

"Nope, it's loose. Hose is fine, but I just need to tighten it. Pass me the gas grips."

"The what?" Tristan questioned, putting his hands up.

"The 'monkey wrench.'"

Tristan quickly reached over to the toolbox and brought him the adjustable wrench whilst taking the fixed wrench back. Charlemagne sat up before bending back over to try and tighten the radiator hose. Tristan looked over to him with anticipation until he finally pulled back up and set the gas grips on his side.

"I think that should do it actually. I may have overlooked everything outside of that. Pass me the pipe so I can put it back inside," Charlemagne said, wiping some sweat from his head as he received the pipe in his opposite hand.

Charlemagne lowered himself again and began to fix the generator pipe. He made the last tugs to ensure it was fastened tight before he raised a smirk on his face. Charlemagne removed his head from overlooking into the tank engine and put both hands on the roof to push himself up. The two of them stood up as he passed the wrench to Tristan and then lowered himself down. Tristan put the wrench into the toolbox and sat down to get off before taking the red toolbox to set it on the floor. Charlemagne closed the rear hatch and then went to a cabinet near the door to fetch the keys.

"Let's hope for the better," Charlemagne told himself as Tristan backed away to the opposite stall to watch.

Charlemagne climbed inside and went into the driver's seat only to realize that his view was blocked by the massive drill in front. However, anxious to know if he finally did it, Charlemagne inserted the keys to start up the engine before climbing up to the switch that engaged the drill. The engine roared to life, giving Charlemagne a wide grin on his face as he held the switch for the drill. He turned the drill on and his smile grew wider as he could hear it rotating and spinning.

Tristan watched and cheered with excitement as a plume of diesel exhaust rose up from behind the tank. Charlemagne climbed up and stood atop the tank. He waved over to Tristan as he showed off his proud smile.

"It's working!" Charlemagne proclaimed. "Now, there is one problem, and that is that the front optics are completely blocked from view," he added with a chuckle, "but I believe that'll be easily correctable if you lead me with the periscope. Other than that, I think...."

A terrible grinding of metal began to overwhelm his voice in the last words of his sentence. Charlemagne was inaudible so he stopped speaking. His smile had turned to a desolate frown as he turned around. Tristan felt the energy in the room quickly shift as the tank gave three terrible shakes before shutting down completely. Smoke lifted up, but not from the exhaust, but the engine.

"Damn!" Charlemagne shouted, smashing a fist on the roof of the tank.

Charlemagne climbed out and jumped down.

"Hey!" Tristan yelled to him.

Charlemagne ignored him and barged past to go back into the cellar and towards the elevator. Tristan gave one look over to the tank before running after Charlemagne as he joined him back upstairs. He continued to pursue him, but Charlemagne had walked quickly away.

"Charles, stop!" Tristan shouted from the foyer as he disappeared into the south wing.

The violent slam of the library doors caught Tristan off-guard, but he persisted. He continued to go forward, into the library, and right to the study. Tristan entered and looked forward as he saw Charlemagne with his head down and palms lined against the front of the desk.

"All my work... all my work for nothing..." Charlemagne told himself in a hushed tone. "I'm an imbecile. I'm a fraud. I can't even get a simple bloody tank to work properly."

"You can never hope to if you take this attitude," Tristan quietly said from the door.

"I've lived all my life in pursuit for the greater things, Tristan," Charlemagne replied, turning to him. "I've lived for so long and done nothing worth the years of life that can be said to be a great and everlasting triumph. I'm no Newton. I'm no Galileo or Da Vinci. I'm not even Thomas Midgley..."

"That's because you're Charlemagne de la Cabernet. You may not have your big breakthrough, but you've got yourself in the books as one of the most notable sons of the Cabernet household. A family legacy that would have had you as a villain, especially if..."

Tristan sighed.

"Especially if you sold the company."

"Thanks, Sal," Charlemagne replied, turning around again.

"No, I'm not like him. I didn't mean to say it, but it is the truth. I didn't care though because I believe you should have been let to do as you saw wished. I don't want this to be one of those conversations though. Charles... I admired you as a scientist. Don't let this failure get you down, because it'll get me down too."

"All it takes is one failure to remind about the sum total of what I am – one big failure," Charlemagne said.

"You have to look past this pessimism. I think the fact that you've failed loads of times is great," Tristan said. "Every great scientist goes through it... we learn more when we fail than when we succeed."

"I've only learned how much a wasted investment my life has come to be. I've wasted the prime years of my own life and missed out on my family, forming my own family, getting an officiated education – a real life like Salmar had. I loved this all, don't get me wrong, but there's something more than what I could have done with my life, and the 'special calling' wasn't for me. I'm not special. I wished and hoped that I was, but I'm not."

"But you're here and you're alive still. It's not too late. You've at least come to learn what's wrong and can turn around. Life isn't about one thing at a time – it's about embracing all of them and being open to all of them to keep ourselves going. It's about doing things, together, with people. Don't be selfish and don't isolate yourself – don't let the image I have of my hero die with you, Charles," Tristan said, going over to him.

Charlemagne turned around and looked over to him as he stood before him. Tristan raised his hand and offered it to him. They looked at each other. Charlemagne with a confused expression and Tristan with a look of pity.

"Diana and I are relying on you. Please, we can fix it together," Tristan offered.

"That's... that's right," Charlemagne replied, shaking Tristan's hand. "I won't let you down," he added.

The two of them made their way back to the stables and went over to the tank. Charlemagne opened the rear hull and looked down at the two cylinders that composed the top of the engine.

"Perhaps it's still the radiator," Charlemagne suggested, taking a look as Tristan got on top.

"If overheating was the problem then it would have blown up," Tristan replied. "What about the fuel pump?"

"The fuel pump? Let me take a look," Charlemagne replied, delving his head to examine the engine. "The fuel pump could explain the sudden shut off."

"I'd say timing belt, but this thing doesn't really have one of those, does it."

"Correct. We have to get this perfect because the last thing we need is for the tank to shut down in the middle of excavating," Charlemagne said, bringing himself back up and putting his tools away.

Tristan got off and took the toolbox with him. Charlemagne on the other hand simply stood up and went over to stand inside the tank while Tristan took his distance.

"Here goes nothing," Charlemagne said as he was about to go.

"Hey," Tristan replied. "In case this doesn't work-"

"I won't give in," Charlemagne instantly replied."

"Okay. Let's do this then."

Charlemagne went down and into the driver's seat to switch on the engine. The Tiger II roared to life and the drill began to spin as it once did mere minutes ago. The two of them held their breath as seconds turned to minutes. Charlemagne got out of the tank and Tristan looked over to him as their anxious faces turned to brief laughter. Charlemagne delved back down to shut the tank off before coming out.

"It works," Charlemagne said with a smile, looking around to think about what was next. "Put that toolbox into that pickup truck for me."

Charlemagne pointed to a grey pickup truck in one of the stables closest to the door. He then went over to the cabinet near the front garage door and took out the keys for the pickup truck. He then went to his sedan and drove it out of the way so he could come back inside and move the truck out. Charlemagne backed it into the pen where there was a platform lying in the mud. He then drove the truck forward and left enough space so that the tank could be driven onto it. From there, he went back to the tank and drove it onto the platform before coming down to meet with Tristan who had gone back upstairs to retrieve his cellphone.

The two of them smiled with a joy that relieved their anxiety to the current situation. The stress of the night turned as they entered the cabin of the pickup truck and began to make their way back to the abandoned coal mine.

Act 5, Scene 2

"What the hell is that thing?" Detective Hudson quietly questioned from his car.

The detective looked out of the front window from his police cruiser to view a pickup truck pulling a tank on a platform behind it.

"Leave it to Charlemagne de la Cabernet," his partner replied, sighting him on the inside of the truck.

Charlemagne pulled the truck into the scene much like he did with his sedan an hour or two ago. He came out of the pickup truck to look at the surprised faces of police officers around the scene.

"Mr. Cabernet!" an officer yelled in defiance to his actions.

Charlemagne didn't listen and instead climbed over to the tank and into the hatch to join Tristan.

"Somebody call the chief right away," another officer said, backing as the tank started its engine.

"No," Hudson rejected, putting his hands to block an officer from contacting Chief Phillips. "Nothing we can do will stop this crazy old fool. Let's just stand back and watch."

The Tiger II roared to life and Charlemagne began to steer himself back gently whilst Tristan stood above, looking through the periscope.

"Gently," Tristan warned as they came off the platform. "Now, take a right, and we're clear."

The tank began to turn and line itself towards the path heading down into the mines.

"Forward," Tristan instructed.

Charlemagne began to accelerate forward. The tank started to run down and come to the bottom of the pit.

"Stop!" Tristan called out.

The tank stopped at the bottom of the dirt ramp.

"Left a little and then straight," Tristan said.

The tank turned left before straightening to line itself towards the rocks blocking the mine entrance.

"This better work," Hudson remarked with a frown as he crossed his arms. "Ready our men to pursue from behind."

"Alright, you've got a clear line! Forward at full-speed for immediate impact!"

Charlemagne began to put his foot down onto the accelerator and the tank began to creep forward slowly before turning to steady pace as it went for the rocks.

Tristan switched the drill on and it began to spin as they made their way forward. At peak velocity, Tristan clenched his teeth for their immediate impact. The tank ripped through the rock, causing a multitude of sounds and scrapes to be heard above and around. The entire vehicle vibrated and slowed down as they dug.

"Brakes!" Tristan alerted, causing Charlemagne to brake immediately.

Tristan saw a black sedan in their immediate path beyond the rocks that began to swerve backwards and out of the path before driving deeper into the caves over their sudden appearance.

"Alright! Go forward!" Tristan said as he looked forward to the mere sentry turrets that began to fire at them.

The tank crushed the automatic turrets with ease, continuing to traverse through the rocky path along the main tunnel, and going downwards and deeper into the cave.

"Oh crap!" Tristan remarked as they accidentally hit a patrol tower and some scaffolding with a mobster atop. "Uh... maybe slow down a little?! Inch to the left too!"

"What?!" Charlemagne questioned.

"Slow down and inch to the left!" Tristan yelled again with more volume. "More!"

"Is that good?"

"Some more! Quickly!" Tristan yelled as they made their descent after the black sedan through a curved tunnel. "Okay! Straight again!"

"Roger," Charlemagne replied, slowing down to properly reposition.

"Speed!" Tristan yelled.

The tank continued down the tunnel and easily crushed over the obstacles of barbed wire and more automatic turret guns. They went further along and finished making a turn around the left and then the right as Tristan began to catch sight of an elevated office. The structure had barred windows and was positioned against a rocky wall at the end of a T-intersection with further tunnels going left and right. Lights could be seen on inside; Tristan was certain that this was where Diana was held up. His confidence that Diana was there grew more and more the closer and closer they got... so much so that it was getting too certain as they got too close!

"Uh... brakes?!" Tristan shouted as they were about a hundred meters from crashing.

"Tristan watched as the mobsters in the sedan got out and abandoned the car in the middle of the path.

"What?!" Charlemagne yelled.

"Brakes!" Tristan shouted again with more volume "Breaks!"

The tank flattened the sedan like a tin can. The bump in the path of running over the car told Charlemagne to slow down.

"Brakes!" Tristan yelled for a fourth time.

Charlemagne slammed on the brakes as they crashed into the first beams holding the office above them. The tank was pelted with the beams of wood above and around them before impacting into the stone in front. Both Tristan and Charlemagne flew forward in their seats. Tristan flinched as a wooden beam came to block the view of the periscope. The vehicle vibrated as it tried to dig into the hard rock in front of them, but it gave up after a few moments before the engine had a meltdown and gave up.

"Are you okay?" Charlemagne asked as he recuperated.

"Yeah... yeah, I'm good," Tristan replied with slight nausea.

Act 5, Scene 3

Louie turned his gaze from the strange large vehicle below and over to Salmar sitting in a chair in the center of the room. Two mobsters entered the office.

"What the hell was that?" Louie asked in reference to the sudden tremors and monstrosity he had just seen.

"A friggin' tank just crashed below," one of them explained.

"A what?" Louie questioned.

"A friggin' tank!"

"You: take Mr. Cabernet. You: come with me," Louie ordered as he pointed to each of them respectively.

"What about the other hostage?" the other asked.

"Forget about 'er. Just get a move on!"

The entire floor of the office began to shake again as the beams below lost their integrity. One of the mobsters quickly grabbed Salmar and began to make their way out before the entire deck collapsed downwards over the tank.

Tristan opened the escape hatch above him as the wreckage settled. He moved his head around to diagnose that the coast was clear. He looked down to Charlemagne below as he made his way out but flinched and jerked his head up as he spotted movement ahead. Some men were coming down the stairwell attached to the office above.

"We've got baddies coming for us," Tristan said to him with both hands at either side of the hatch.

Go! Hide! Quickly!" Charlemagne ordered as he looked up.

Tristan quickly backed up as they set foot at the bottom of the staircase. He hid along the side of the tank until he spotted a shack up ahead at the dead-end of the right-turn from the main tunnel. He ran over to hide behind the far-side. Tristan turned around to look over as he noticed that there were only three mobsters with one hostage: Salmar, and now two, including Charlemagne.

"Diana?" Tristan whispered to himself as the pack began to go forward down the tunnel.

Tristan looked around and saw nothing but the rocky tunnel of the mine he was in. Once he felt sure that the mobsters ahead were far enough for him to come out, he stood up from his crouch and patted his shorts and sweater. He began to step forward to follow the crooks, but quickly stepped back as he heard the creak of the wooden structure giving in to gravity.

The office collapsed, forcing Tristan back to take cover again. He coughed and hacked as the dust approached him. He rested his hand against the side of the shack and looked into the window to notice Diana inside, tied to a chair with no mobsters keeping watch. Tristan coughed again before picking up his morale as he put his other hand on the glass to look over to Diana who had her head down.

"Diana!" Tristan shouted with a surreal level of happiness.

"Tristan?" Diana questioned, picking up her head and looking out to Tristan. "Tristan!"

Tristan quickly came around and through the wooden door of the shack as a little more debris fell from above. Tristan smiled to Diana, who was still dressed in her grass skirt and tank top.

"You took your freaking time," Diana remarked as Tristan rushed her.

"Sorry, we had some technical problems," Tristan replied as he untied her.

"What's with all the noise out there?" Diana questioned as she brought her arms back in front of her.

"It's a long story that involves a tank and Charlemagne's bad driving," Tristan quickly replied, standing up as Diana was free.

"Charlemagne?" Diana questioned as she got up and rubbed her wrists.

"Yeah. Thanks to him, we – well, I'm here to rescue you."

"Where is he now?" Diana asked as they started to move out.

"He, uh... just got captured."

"Nice," Diana sarcastically remarked as they stopped in front of the door. "What do we do now?"

"Now? We've got to go after him! They've got Sal and Charles and just went down the tunnel."

"Then let's go!" Diana replied, running out and around the mess of debris.

Tristan ran after her, and the two ran together as they followed the mine rail tracks further down the tunnel. The tunnel began to slope downwards again before stretching for another kilometer and then ending.

"What now?" Tristan commented as they nearly arrived at the dead-end.

"Over here," Diana replied, nudging Tristan and pointing towards a small trench in an enclave ahead.

The pair rushed over and looked down to see water running in one direction, away from them.

"Lady's first," Diana joked, pushing Tristan into the stream of water.

Diana jumped in after him and looked over to Tristan on the floor as he got himself up. Diana went over to help him up.

"Thanks," Tristan said in a sarcastic tone.

"Don't be such a wuss," Diana remarked as they looked between the two directions they could go. "Where to now?"

The tunnel was narrow and cylindrical. They were effectively in a large pipe.

"Now?" Tristan questioned, taking his cell phone from his pocket. "Now, I send the cops our location, because I forgot to do so earlier and my battery is almost dead. I'd have thought they'd be behind us..."

Tristan unlocked his phone and tapped an emergency setting that transmitted his location.

"We should wait for them now that we know which way they took Charlemagne," Tristan said as Diana got a head start.

"Or, we could move along to make sure we're still actively behind them," Diana replied. "I mean, wait for the coppers? No thanks. I've done enough waiting for those bozos."

"Diana..." Tristan complained, walking down the stream of water to go after her.

The pair of them walked for almost an hour before they heard an echo further ahead that said in an Italian-American accent, "I'm going to enjoy putting you down! Now get down there!"

Diana turned to Tristan as he caught up to her. The two of them looked at each other before they continued side by side down the one-way route. Within five minutes they arrived at the end of the pipe tunnel and entered a large and spacious room with metal catwalks, flooring, and an assortment of pipes along the walls and ceiling. Below was a single, wide canal where the flow of water dropped to reach a calm river flowing downwards, or forward. A smooth metal floor could be seen on either side, but the drop from the pipe they were in and into the shallow water was steep.

"Keep your mouth shut!" a mobster yelled from somewhere ahead.

"Lower me down, will you?" Diana asked, lowering her feet and offering her hand to Tristan.

Tristan grabbed her hand and began to lower Diana down as much as he could before she'd have to drop. Diana let go at a suitable height and splashed down.

"Alright, your turn," Diana replied, waving to him.

Tristan got on his knees and lowered himself with his torso before extending his arms, hands and fingers. His grip on the pipe was poor, caused him to lose grip and fall downwards. He landed in the pool of shallow water on his side. Diana went over to help him up. Tristan got up and raised his head to look forward. The canal was immediately cut-off by a blast door ahead, forcing excess water to take grates on either side in the walls left and right.

"Come on, let's go," Diana said to him, holding his arm as they went to a ladder.

The two of them climbed up to the edge of the canal.

"I hate getting wet when I'm not expecting it," Tristan whined over the coldness of all the water absorbed into his clothing.

"At least you're actually wearing something appropriate," Diana retaliated in discomfort of her skirt.

"Why don't you abandon that thing – aren't you wearing shorts underneath?"

"I haven't had the time to," Diana replied, taking the skirt off. "It seems a shame to leave it behind – it's not even mine."

"Yeah, well, you can come pick it up later," Tristan responded. "Come on, let's keep moving."

The two of them froze as they looked at the metal staircase going up and then down to go over to another room. A blue-suited mafia member came up and stood atop the staircase with his Thompson machine gun pointed at them.

"Well, lookie what we gots here," the deep voice said to them. "Hands up, kiddos. Nice and up so I can see them."

The crook walked down the stairs with the gun pointed at them. Tristan and Diana both raised their hands. The mobster walked a few feet away from the base of the stairs and then used the barrel of the submachine gun to point where he wanted them to go. The pair went forward and up the stairs to come atop and look down at the other side where the other mobsters were with their guns pointed down into the empty trench on the other side where Salmar and Charlemagne were both inside and on their knees. Both adults looked up and towards the kids.

"You brought my kid with you?" Salmar questioned to Charlemagne.

"He volunteered," Charlemagne argued, looking back to him.

"Ain't this nice? Always nice to have the family together," Louie commented, pointing to the other to send the kids down.

Diana and Tristan were brought to the edge of the canal where they were directed to go downwards to join their guardians.

"Come on. Down you go," the mobster said, tapping the side of the barrel of the gun into their backs.

Tristan hesitated to jump into what would certainly be death. He grabbed Diana's arm as he felt the stress rise. The mobsters didn't tolerate their insolence and pushed them in.

Charlemagne looked over to the kids as they fell in. He began to feel remorse.

"Oh, how could I have let two youngsters get involved in this," Charlemagne said. "We're all going to die by my hand.... Tristan, why didn't you escape when you found Diana?"

Charlemagne looked to Tristan as he waited for an answer. Tristan got up as he looked at Charlemagne and couldn't answer.

"I didn't want to leave you behind," Diana replied instead, behind him. "Either of you."

"Shut it," Louie ordered to them, pointing his gun down and signaling his friend on the other side. "Raise the flood gates and let's get the water flowing so we can get out of here. This has gone on long enough."

"Why are you doing this?" Charlemagne questioned. "Do you want money? I can give you money!"

"Sorry, Mr. Cabernet, but we're bought and paid for already. Besides, we got a reputation to keep up, you know? We have to honor the agreement we made for the sake of the Medici family name, right? Now, don't you worry. We're going to make this thing speed up now and it'll all be over. We'll get the water started, fire our guns at you, and then let the water take your corpses down the drain. Easy peasy."

The blast doors on either side of them began to open. Water began to flow down the canal and trickle along their feet. Water also began to spill into the canal from pipe outlets behind them. Louie looked down at them in spite as the water slowly increased in velocity and depth.

"Raise the speed, will ya? Not too much though. You know the plan," Louie ordered, looking over to another mobster behind him. "Get on that other valve! They'll be nothing but a trio of corpses."

"You got it, boss," he replied, going over to take control of a second valve.

"You've got me..." Charlemagne said, "so let the kids and my brother go, please! The cops already know that you're behind this so taking care of loose ends is pointless!"

"True, true... but I can never be too careful, can I?" Louie assured him, kneeling down on one knee and looking over to them. "This, err... work of ours is a specialty, and 'loose ends' need to be dealt with accordingly with precious. I can't just..."

"Boss?" a mobster yelled from the other side, letting go of the valve with a quick spin as he raised his machine gun. "Ah!"

The gangster was shot in the arm.

"Freeze! Police!" a cop shouted from nearby.

"Aw crap!" Louie yelled. "You see? Take cover. Raise the water!"

Charlemagne stood up as the water began to turn further up in speed. He looked over to the nearest ladder where Salmar was making his way over. Salmar fell over with the sheer force of a heavy wave that knocked everybody aside. Tristan looked over to Diana as gunfire echoed above them and the increased flow caused a harder wave to tackle against them.

"I can't swim!" Diana yelled as the water got to her chest.

Salmar struggled at the ladder. Tristan waded against the flow and grabbed Diana by her waist as Salmar recuperated and began to climb up.

"Let's go," Charlemagne said, moving over to the teens so they can make their way to and up the ladder after Salmar.

Another rough wave began to flow down, causing Tristan to pull Diana closer as they were knocked over and submerged slightly. Charlemagne fell over too. A third wave came not too soon after the second, hitting Salmar back into the water and peaking on the fourth in a brutal rapid that was too much for all of them. Charlemagne swam up as they started to quickly travel down and away from the scene. He briefly watched as the police closed in on one mobster before being forced again to travel to wherever the water took the four of them.

Act 5, Scene 4

The torrential flush of water dragged the family through a narrow tunnel. Tristan held tight to Diana but the cruelty in the rapids started to drag them apart until he could no longer hold on to her and had to let go. Charlemagne opened his eyes as he caught a breath of air and made his way up before closing his eyes and mouth with a pocket of air as he was dragged down again.

A large pipe tunnel spat the four of them out and into a calm pool in a larger room. Charlemagne floated in the water before straightening up and struggling to catch himself. He coughed over the water in his lungs before he swam over to Diana as she floated around. Charlemagne put his arms around her and quickly swam over to a grated platform to pull her lifeless body over. Diana began to fidget and hack loudly before rolling onto her side to vomit the excess water out. Charlemagne pulled himself up and began to look around for Tristan and his brother.

Salmar managed to have stayed conscious and began to swim over to an opposite platform around the catwalk.

"Where's Tristan?" Diana questioned, kneeling over the platform and looking for him.

"I don't know," Charlemagne quietly replied. "Let's go up for a better look."

Charlemagne stood up and walked over the ladder besides them to go higher up to the main platform. He let Diana up first before he went up behind. Diana pressed herself against the ledge to look around for Tristan. Charlemagne joined her and searched. He then turned around to look over to Salmar as he was bent over on the opposite-side with his hands on his knees and in a heavy cough. The two of them, Diana and

Charlemagne, continued to search carefully for anywhere that Tristan might be.

"No..." Charlemagne confessed in fear of having lost Tristan.

Charlemagne gave a quick look over to Diana and her strange expression of worry and loss. He then turned his gaze behind to see what was going on.

"What are you doing?" Charlemagne reacted, dropping a frown at Salmar. "Tristan..."

"Will be missed," Salmar confessed.

Salmar held one hand at his side and another around the handle of a pistol that he pointed towards the two of them.

"I'm ending this once and for all," Salmar remarked with a wide frown, bloodshot eyes, and wet hair. "All I wanted was for you to stop selling the company, and I tried, but you've forced me to resort to extreme measures. So much is at stake, Charles. You don't understand. You never understood. I tried to get you to understand, but I wasn't even able to hire a couple of Italian morons to kill you! No less – I had to get myself kidnapped, flushed down the sewer and dropped into this dump. I'm sick of it! I've lost my patience – and to be honest, I should have probably have just done this from the start!"

"Why?" Charlemagne remarked. "Why do all of this?"

"Because Cabernet Industries is *mine*, Charles! It's mine!" Salmar explained. "I'm tired of living under your shadow! For forty-five years I've had to dwell with your scavenges, your spotlight, your exposure on the media – Charlemagne the Scientist... Charlemagne the Explorer... Charlemagne the Innovator – because there could be only one great and magnificent son of Everest de la Cabernet, which left me as Salmar... the boring and insignificant lawyer. Did you think I cared if you lived or not? I never loved you... but when I heard that you were going to throw the legacy away instead of handing it over to me... of course I had to act. It's mine and I won't have some foreigners rubbing their hands around what is mine!"

"You sold your shares to me. It was your own fault that you were cut-out of the corporation – the family's corporation. Father left all three of us with equal shares. However, you were naïve and impatient," Charlemagne retaliated, inching to the side so he was closer to Diana.

"I can't believe you *let* me sell my shares to you. You practically put the idea into my head! It's your fault!"

"Salmar..." Charlemagne replied.

"Shut up!" Salmar responded, firing the gun and causing Charlemagne to flinch as the bullet flew past.

The hissing of steam echoed in the chamber. Diana looked over to Salmar with a frown. She looked down at her feet, through the steel grate flooring and down to the water below as she hoped to see Tristan.

"I hired the Medici family to do one job tonight and that was to kill you. I paid them good money too (my hard-earned savings), but I must admit that it's true... if you really want something done, then you've just got to do it yourself... even if that means getting your own hands dirty."

"I can't believe this," Charlemagne sneered. "This is all a dramatization. I was *never* the tremendous son of the Cabernet family you think me to be. I was always the outcast that had to find my own way to happiness because I had been rejected by society around me. You had a normal life. You had a wife-"

"Gloria died!" Salmar shouted back.

"And you could have moved on as you were!" Charlemagne retaliated. "No less... with the child you adopted."

"It's too late for that though... Those police can arrest the mobsters, but by the time they come around here, you'll be a dead man and I'll be a rich man. Say goodbye, my dear brother," Salmar said, raising his gun back up and aiming for Charlemagne. "This is my present from me, to you, on your birthday – the death that you've longed for so long."

Diana clenched her teeth in anxiety as Salmar pointed the gun towards Charlemagne. She rapped a fist around the metal railing behind her as she braced for her turn.

Charlemagne looked over to his brother in fear, but also a dissociated sense of betrayal with no surprise.

"Go ahead," Charlemagne said, looking over to him with a straight eye. "Take your best shot."

Salmar tensed his finger around the trigger as Charlemagne prepared to defend Diana. Instantly, a large clank of metal could be heard instead of a gunshot as Tristan jumped from the ladder behind Salmar with a pipe in hand. Salmar jumped and fired the gun out of fear and into the pipe above him as he turned around.

"Aaah!" Salmar yelled as steam sprayed into his face.

Tristan swung the pipe at him as he dropped the gun, causing him to be knocked to the side as he fell unconscious with a reddened face. Tristan looked at him before throwing the pipe aside as the steam dissipated. He looked over to Charlemagne and Diana as they looked back at him with surprise and shock in their faces.

"Police!" a voice yelled from the distance.

"Over here!" Charlemagne shouted, turning to Diana as he put a hand on her shoulder. "Are you alright?"

Tristan walked over to the two as Diana looked up to Charlemagne.

"Yeah, I'm, uh... I'm okay," Diana replied, looking back over to Salmar's unconscious body on the floor.

Charlemagne put his other hand on Tristan's shoulder as he looked at him with concern.

"Are you alright as well?" he asked.

"I'm fine," Tristan replied.

The three of them looked over to the police as they arrived.

"Detain him!" Charlemagne remarked, pointing to his brother as he let go from both kids. "Retrieve the weapon as evidence – he tried to murder us."

The officers crowded around Charlemagne as another radioed for paramedics. Another two police officers escorted the others out of the water facility and to the surface parking lot. They had made it to the outskirts of town and were at the Nattau Water Treatment Facility.

•

Minutes had passed and the night had ended when an ambulance finally arrived to assist the three. Additional police cruisers came along with them. Sunlight poured in from the east behind the water treatment facility as it was early morning.

A paramedic ran over to the kids before coming to Charlemagne. Salmar, who had awakened, was being forced into a police cruiser away from them. He was silent.

"Looks like your wrist is okay, Mr. Cabernet," a paramedic concluded after a careful examination.

"Good to hear," Charlemagne replied, lowering his sleeve and turning to the police officers as he had just finished giving them his statement. "Anything else I can help you with?"

"No, Charles, that'll be all," Detective Hudson replied, closing his notebook and putting it away into his blazer. "You're good to go. Get some rest and take care."

Charlemagne nodded to him as he stood up from the stretcher. He walked away from the ambulance and slowly made his way towards the mess of police cruisers ahead near the entrance of the parking lot. Despite it being the start of a new day, Charlemagne looked to be alert with open eyes and a light smile on his face as he looked around the scene.

"Mr. Cabernet!" a familiar voice yelled.

Charlemagne spun around to find the source of the voice before meeting with a balding man in a brown suit.

"I've got great news, Mr. Cabernet!"

"Oh?" Charlemagne questioned, smiling and putting his hands behind his back. "Let's hear it."

"All the paperwork is complete and we're ready to take Diana Cambridge with us to a temporary foster home."

"Oh..." Charlemagne replied, dropping his excitement and smile.

"It was tough – but I managed to find someone that I believe will be *just* right for her. This home specializes in rebellious youth like her and there are plenty more of them for her to get along with," Gregson boasted.

"I see," Charlemagne simply replied, looking past him and over to the rear of an ambulance where he saw Tristan with Diana.

Each of them smiled as they sat together and rested at the step of the ambulance rear. They had emergency blankets on and were deep in a conversation.

"Where is she?" Gregson queried, looking around.

"She's, uh... she's not going anywhere," Charlemagne concluded after a quick thought. "I'm not giving her up."

"What?" Gregson responded, looking at him with an annoyed face. "But I did all the paperwork, and I... I..."

"And you did a great job and I'll be more than willing to pay for any time lost. In the meantime, I have changed my opinion and would like her to remain in my care for the better," Charlemagne assured him with a warm smile as he brought an arm around his shoulder and started to walk him away.

"If that's the case, then I suppose I'll take the other then," Gregson sighed, pushing Charlemagne off as he turned to him.

"The other?" Charlemagne questioned.

"I was actually here by coincidence. Chief Phillips called me about another boy – that one over there," Gregson said, pointing over to Tristan.

"Tristan?" Charlemagne replied. "No. You can't have him either."

"What?" Gregson responded, looking to him.

"Tristan is staying with me too – I demand guardianship and full custody. He was the son of my brother, and it is only fair that I as next of kin foster and adopt him."

"Uh..." Gregson hesitated. "I don't know..."

"Come on, Mr. Gregson," Charlemagne insisted, patting him on the shoulder. "Surely such a request would save you loads of time in searching for a foster home on such short notice. I'm giving you a great offer – I am next of him, after all."

"That's right," Gregson replied. "This is a better option – a little unexpected, but better. I could start the paperwork so you can adopt him as soon as I get back to the office."

"Ahah! You see!" Charlemagne praised as they began to walk over to the kids. "I wouldn't have this any other way!"

Diana looked away from Tristan and towards the adults as they approached them. Diana grew a frown from her smile as she recognized Mr. Gregson. Tristan noticed the change in expression and looked over to the adults.

"Hello there," Charlemagne said, smiling as he stopped in front of them. "How are you both doing health-wise?"

"Paramedic said we were both alright," Diana replied. "Is he... is he here to take me away?" she asked in reference to Mr. Gregson and Charlemagne's wide smile on his face.

"No, quite the contrary," Gregson replied, holding his clipboard at hand. "I was coming to pick up Mr. Merrick here," he explained, looking over to him, "but Mr. Cabernet here has made sure that the two of you won't be going anywhere else..."

"What do you mean?" Tristan questioned.

"What I mean is, is that Mr. Cabernet will be your new guardian, Tristan. He's both your guardian."

"What?" Diana questioned. "Really? What about me?"

"You too," Gregson replied.

"Yes," Charlemagne replied, confirming it, "and I know I've been awful and terribly rude these past two months – there is no excuse for my selfish actions, but instead, perhaps, not penance, but a gesture of peace. I do not want this forced upon you, Diana. I understand your situation (where you come from) and all the rest, so I do not want to force this upon you. However, nor do I wish to separate the two of you since... well, I'll just get down to it. I want the choice to be yours because I'm offering you a home at the manor. I'm no father, but I am extending my hands to attempt to be an adoptive one. What do you say?"

"I..." Diana hesitated for a moment. "I guess I have no choice."

"No, the choice *is* yours," Charlemagne reaffirmed.

"Then I accept," Diana replied, looking over to Tristan as he smiled at her.

"Perfect," Mr. Gregson responded. "I'll leave you three then and I'll be in touch with you, Charlemagne, with the process of adopting Tristan."

"Very good. Thank you, Mr. Gregson," Charlemagne thanked, turning to him as he left.

"Why the change of heart?" Diana questioned as the social worker was now gone.

"I could ask you the same question," he replied, looking to her before Tristan. "Tristan," he said, "I am deeply sorry about Salmar."

"Don't be," Tristan replied. "I'm just happy that it's all over and that I'll have a home to stay – no less with you – both of you."

"Thank you," Charlemagne said, gesturing to them to stand up. "I can't offer much as a man, but a home is a home, and I promise that you'll never have a reason to not call the manor a place that is yours. I... I feel anew after all that's happened. I also feel a refreshed desire to invent again and see the world as a newborn man – you won't regret your decisions to stay. No, because together we're going to experience a world like no other and I'll be sure that you will feel the happiness I have pursued since I was your age. Together, we're going to have lots of adventures and you will come to experience and see the world in a different light."

Diana and Tristan smiled to Charlemagne before he dropped his sight to the ground and then smiled to them.

"Come now," Charlemagne said, gesturing them to stand, "and let's go to your new home."

The trio left the rear of the ambulance and met up with Detective Hudson who took them with him back to the abandoned mine, and from there, Charlemagne drove the kids back to the mansion in the grey pickup truck.

Charlemagne had felt a great sense of innovation within him. The next hours did not proceed with him falling asleep, but instead with him retrieving his excavator from the mines and going so far as to a period of brainstorming in his study where he would later fall asleep on his desk from exhaustion. He had meant every word he had offered his adopted children.

Over the last two months, he had been a failure as a parent and a man to Diana. He cared nothing but for himself in those moments. However, that time had passed with the rush of this latest adventure – but it wasn't the adventure alone, but who he had spent it with, children of the next generation. Now, he wasn't out to be a parent out of pity even, but instead a parent for the sake of being called into parenthood. His life came after there's, and from now on, there's were with him on to adventure. To teach them. To enlighten them. To love them. To be as any parent should be to their child: an instructor and guardian in the brave new world a child is thrown into where they will search for meaning and truth, and for the upmost level of happiness, the essence of happiness itself – ultimate happiness – the fourth level.

Epilogue

"Mr. Cabernet!" Richard greeted at the rear entrance of the Cabernet research facility on the outskirts of Allabrese.

Charlemagne got out of his car and walked over to the tall, light-brown haired man in a posh black suit with an open-button ruby red dress shirt. He extended his arms out with an exciting smile and embraced his old friend.

"Richard!" Charlemagne greeted in return, parting from him as they started to make their way through the rear doors of the science center. "What have you called me for?"

"I only wanted to know if you were well. I haven't heard from you since last night! Was everything okay at your birthday party?"

"Oh, it was quite a scene, but everything is okay now," Charlemagne replied as they entered the darkness of the receiving garage to escape the summer heat. "However, I must admit that it was more than a fantastic birthday thanks to my kids."

"Kids? I'm glad to hear," Richard replied with a hint of curiosity and suspicion.

"Anyways... more on that later. You can catch it all in the news, I'm sure of it. Journalists were wild at the gates of the manor wanting to know what was going on. Most of them from Harlech than anywhere else."

"Yes, I'm sure it's made a great headline as you're used to by now."

"I'm glad you called me for that. I was going to call later this evening, but I had fallen asleep until you called. I need you to cancel all negotiations and tell our attorneys to scrap every last deal made in the last month in the purchase of any of our assets."

"Sir?" Richard questioned. "Are you sure?"

"I'm one hundred percent positive, Richard," Charlemagne assured, turning to him as they stopped in the middle of a corridor. "Now, instead we've got great things to do with this company. This news will surely send shares up again."

"I'm sure it will. We've been sitting down at an all-time low with 'rumors' of disbandment."

"All but rumors as of now. No, instead, we're going back in business."

"Very good to hear, sir," Richard replied, smiling before they continued to walk together through the facility.

Charlemagne smiled to himself before he looked at his wristwatch.

"Anyways, I've got to go. The kids will be waking up soon and I wouldn't want to leave them alone after all that's happened. A new life will need to be surged through the mansion, and I'm sure they've got a hundred new ideas on how to spruce the place up since it's been a literal tomb for this half of the year."

"Very well," Richard replied as Charlemagne pulled away.

"Take care, Richard," Charlemagne said, waving to him before heading back down the tunnel to go to his car.

"Oh, and sir?!" Richard questioned, causing Charlemagne to turn around again.

"Yes?"

"I have just one question, sir. Did this Mr. Gregson ever find out how Diana came to your care? It bothers me to know."

"No idea!" Charlemagne replied with a carefree smile. "Frankly, it hasn't bothered me since my birthday and shan't ever again! Adieu, old friend!"

"It's good to have you back, sir," Richard said with a nod and smile.

Charlemagne nodded in humor and smiled. He continued down the hall and made his way back to the shipping and receiving area, but not before passing two technicians that passed him in steel blue jumpsuits, tinted orange goggles, and white hardhats.

"I can't believe we're being sent into those tunnels again," one of them remarked as they passed Charlemagne.

"Oh, please," the other replied as they walked down the tunnel. "What are you? Afraid of ghosts or something?

Charlemagne turned to them and then continued walking forward as he reached the doors to shipping and receiving. He paused for a moment, turned his head back down the tunnel towards the technicians and noticed that they were gone. His mouth opened in shock, but quickly closed as he tensed his face with assurance and doubt. He left the corridor and went back to his car without another thought to it.

"Good parents are good parents, for instance, only if their first concern is their children's goodness, not their own."

– Peter Kreeft